"Don't you get it, Nadine? I like *you*."

She couldn't breathe. How tall was this mountain? Was it high altitude or something? What had happened to all of the oxygen in the air?

"And this." Zach kissed her, his mouth meeting hers before she could turn away, hard and soft, cool and hot. Or maybe she didn't want to turn away.

She sank into him, curled into his arms, delved into his mouth with her tongue and savored him in this private little cocoon of theirs.

Nadine had wanted this. For a long time, she had wanted this. How had she not realized that she'd wanted *him*?

A tendril of reason, the finest filigree of common sense, tickled her judgment, and she pulled her lips away from Zach's beautiful, ravenous mouth.

No, *ravenous* wasn't right. He hadn't demanded. He hadn't lost control. He had savored and adored her lips.

She traced his finely sculpted mouth with her finger, met his passion-hazed gaze and said, "No."

Dear Reader,

More and more, with each new story I set in Rodeo, Montana, this miniseries becomes my favorite. I delight in the characters and the caring women who want to bring their town back to life with the revival of their local fair and rodeo. If along the way they find love...even better!

In New York City, Nadine Campbell had a busy career as a journalist and no time for love. Recently, her career suffered a harrowing setback and she has come home to lick her wounds.

Zach Brandt has appeared throughout this series as a landscape artist. His paintings grace many of the establishments in and around Rodeo. First and foremost, though, he is a rancher. His love of the land moves him to create his artwork and sustains him through hard times.

In high school, he had a crush on Nadine Campbell and is happy that she is back in town. Could he have a second chance with her? She has come home a changed woman.

A divorced father of seven-year-old twin sons, Zach uses their cute antics to his advantage to get Nadine out onto his ranch as often as he can. He shows her all of his love and compassion to help her to heal and to win her heart.

Of course, the road to a happy ending is never smooth!

I hope you enjoy this latest story about Rodeo.

Mary Sullivan

RODEO FAMILY

———

MARY SULLIVAN

HARLEQUIN® WESTERN ROMANCE

Recycling programs
for this product may
not exist in your area.

ISBN-13: 978-1-335-69969-5

Rodeo Family

Copyright © 2018 by Mary Sullivan

Printed in U.S.A.

Mary Sullivan has a fondness for cowboys and ranch settings. She grew up in the city, but found her mother's stories about growing up in rural Canada fascinating. Her passions include time spent with friends, great conversation, exploring her city, cooking, walking, traveling (including her latest trip to Paris!), reading, meeting readers and doing endless crossword puzzles. She has been told that her writing touches the heart. Mary loves to hear from readers! To keep up with her releases, sign up for her newsletter on her website, marysullivanbooks.com, or follow her on Facebook: Facebook.com/marysullivanauthor.

Books by Mary Sullivan

Harlequin Western Romance

Rodeo, Montana

Rodeo Father
Rodeo Rancher
Rodeo Baby
Rodeo Sheriff

Harlequin Superromance

Cody's Come Home
Safe in Noah's Arms
No Ordinary Home

Visit the Author Profile page
at Harlequin.com for more titles.

To Jennifer Hayward and Stefanie London,
thank you for your friendship, your brainstorming
and our fabulous weekly walks and talks!

Chapter One

Zachary Brandt wasn't a coward.

Not usually.

He hovered behind a curtain at the picture window that looked out onto his front yard as Nadine Campbell drove her sporty little black car onto his ranch.

In rural Montana on the outskirts of small-town Rodeo, home of dusty, domestic, practical pickup trucks, Nadine scooted around the countryside in her spotless, foreign car.

He should be out on his porch in full view to greet her, not hiding here inside, building up his resolve.

She parked, adjusted her rearview mirror and fiddled with her makeup, the gesture speaking of insecurity he'd noted in the past.

Even way back in high school, before she'd left town for those eight or so years, she'd been self-conscious about her looks. Zach couldn't imagine why, or what she was doing to makeup that was never less than perfect.

She smoothed her long, red hair, as glossy as glass. Nadine belonged in Rodeo about as much as a racehorse might, an elegant, refined filly among a bunch of stolid workhorses.

"Whatcha doin', Dad?"

Zach startled. No wonder. He'd just been caught spy-

ing on a visitor rather than stepping outside to welcome
her. He glanced over his shoulder. His twin sons stood
in the living room doorway. They weren't the only ones
who'd caught him; Zach's father had, too.

Dad raised an eyebrow. Ryan and Aiden watched
him with Maria's deep brown eyes and wide, full-lipped
mouths. She might not have left Zach with much, but
she'd given him these two treasures and for that he would
always be grateful.

They stepped forward and crowded him at the window. Staring out at Nadine, Aiden whispered, "Pretty."

Understatement. Nadine could give lessons in *pretty*
to the Montana countryside, and Zach thought that was
damned stunning.

"Who is she, Dad?" Ryan asked.

"Her name is Nadine Campbell, and she's a reporter
for the newspaper."

"I saw her before in town," Aiden said. "She's got
red hair."

As red as red could be.

"What's she doing here?" That was Ryan, as curious as ever.

"She's going to interview me."

Ryan looked up, not as far as he used to. His kids
were growing too fast. Seven years old already. "What
about? Our ranch?"

"Partly. She wants to talk about my paintings, but they
wouldn't exist without the ranch. Right?"

"Right," Ryan answered. He'd heard it all from his
dad before, about how his paintings were an outward expression of his love of his land. Then a knowing smile
lit his face. "But you're gonna get her to talk about the
ranch!"

Zach ruffled his hair. "You're too smart to be a kid. Are you an adult in disguise?"

Ryan pressed into his hand.

Zach's quiet son, Aiden, stood in front of him, leaning back against his legs. Zach settled a hand on his shoulder.

Nadine's car door opened. He didn't want to be caught staring. "Come away from the window." He tried to herd them from the room, but Dad stepped brazenly in front of the window with a mischievous smile hovering on his lips.

"Nadine Campbell." Zach's father pretended to think, but his eyes sparkled. "Hmm. Name sounds familiar."

"Of course it's familiar," Zach snapped. "You know everyone in town." His dad's feigned ignorance didn't fool him. The man knew who Nadine was. Did he realize what she used to mean to Zach?

Did he realize what she could still mean to him if Zach had his way?

Second chances rarely happened in real life. Sometimes a man had to grasp that second chance with both hands before it slipped away. A determined man did, at any rate. Zach had managed to spend years, long swathes of time, forgetting about Nadine, but here she was back on his ranch.

"I remember her from years ago before she left town," Dad said.

Maybe Dad had known how Zach had felt. He could be intuitive...when it suited him.

"She stood out, back then," Dad said.

"Pop, let's go," Zach insisted, trying to get his father to step away from the window. "Get away from there."

Aiden shrugged off Zach's hand on his shoulder and joined his grandfather at the window. Ryan did the same thing.

"She's getting out of the car!" Ryan shouted.

"Modulate, Ryan," Zach said.

"She's got pretty shoes on," Aiden whispered.

Aiden spoke too low. Ryan lived at full volume. If only Zach could even them out. On second thought, no. Each was perfect in his own way.

"Those shoes will get wrecked," Pop said.

A thought occurred to Zach. "How come you remember her from when she was a teenager?"

His father pretended to look surprised. What game was he playing? "She came out here once with a bunch of kids when you were in high school, for some project or other."

"Yes, she did." Zach remembered that visit with vivid discomfort.

"She didn't like the ranch," Pop said, bringing back Zach's disappointment.

It had hurt his teenage ego. The ranch had been, and still was, his world. His pride and joy.

Aiden tugged on his sleeve. "They'll get wrecked, Dad."

"Those shoes? Sure will. You two," he said, touching their heads, "root through the rubber boots in the back porch and see if you can find a pair that might fit our guest."

Maria's would still be back there. She sure wouldn't have taken reminders of the ranch with her, and Zach hadn't cleared out the porch in the three years since she'd left.

The boys ran off toward the back of the house.

Pop turned from the window. "Didn't she used to have a mess of curly hair to her waist?"

Yes, her hair had been a mass of long, red curls. Her face had sported more freckles than Zach could ever hope to count. Where had those gone, both the curls and the freckles? How did a person change her appearance so drastically?

Zach eyed his father. "I don't remember you having a photographic memory."

"She stood out," he said, "'cause I knew you liked her. I paid attention. Wanted to make sure she was worthy of my son. She didn't like the ranch. End of story."

Pop had known he'd liked her? And he'd worried about Zach? It warmed him.

Nadine still stood out, just in a different shell than the one she used to wear. And hadn't he always wanted to get a good long look inside that shell?

Dad watched him altogether too carefully before raising that pesky eyebrow again and murmuring, "Well."

Yes. Well. Some feelings died over time, but some only pretended to, living underground and flaring back to the surface the second a woman came back to town after years away. When she had returned a year ago, he'd been shocked. After high school, she'd told anyone who would listen that she was heading off to New York City to meet her destiny. To forge a career on television.

Now she was back and no one knew why. She didn't seem to have plans to leave. Zach hoped that would work in his favor. But obviously too much showed on his face if Dad, in his oblique way, was commenting on it. Zach wiped his expression clear of emotion and stepped out onto the veranda.

Lee Beeton, owner of the *Rodeo Wrangler*, had pestered Zach for an interview for years. Zach had said no. Then Nadine had come back to Rodeo. A year later, she'd asked for an interview. Zach had said yes.

A second chance…

Would she like the ranch any better this time? Would she like him?

She stretched her slim legs, her pretty high heels emphasizing their length while she rummaged in her purse. She didn't belong here. Their differences struck him anew. *I am a sturdy Clydesdale and she is an exquisite Arabian.*

He crossed his arms. Why was it taking her so long to get out of one small car?

And what's the rush, Zach? You aren't usually this impatient.

Yeah, but Nadine had come back to his ranch.

NADINE CAMPBELL COULDN'T delay her meeting with Zach Brandt any longer. She had to get out of this car. She had to face him down.

What had started as a simple story about Zach's love of the landscape and painting it, a story she had looked forward to writing, had turned into a snafu of huge proportions just this morning.

Nadine did not want to be here. There was no way out. Trapped, panic clogged her throat. Could a person suffocate on anger?

Her nerves rattled like a pair of castanets. She shouldn't have stopped in at the newspaper office before coming out for the interview. Then she wouldn't have seen her boss, Lee Beeton, who wouldn't have put her into this awful, awful bind.

Find out that family's secrets.

No. That wasn't Nadine's job. Her job was to talk to Zach about his artwork. That's it. Nothing else. No digging up dirt. What was Lee's purpose in needing to know secrets anyway? He didn't publish a gossip rag.

But he'd issued an ultimatum—do it or you're fired—

and now she had no choice but to write the story he wanted.

In the brilliant sunshine bathing Zach's ranch, Nadine felt clunky and awkward, an old feeling she'd thought she'd outgrown. With this awful new directive from Lee, any smooth confidence she might have possessed had deserted her this morning. She ran a hand over her twitchy stomach.

From the car, she retrieved the canvas bag that contained the tools of her trade: notepad, laptop, recording device, pencils and pens. The bag was her raison d'être. Her security blanket, its very existence reminded her that, yes indeed, she was a bona fide journalist who deserved to be writing.

She sensed Zach's presence on his veranda. She couldn't avoid him any longer, so she turned and walked toward the house.

He stood on his porch steps and watched her approach with his unnerving steady regard. Did the man never blink?

The ranch hadn't changed since her tour here in high school for a project about local cattle ranching. The sturdy white brick house with blue shutters might be considered by some to be pretty. There was nothing wrong with it, but it wasn't to her taste. She liked modern and sleek. Not that she found much of either here in Rodeo, but back in New York City—oh, heavenly, perfect New York—there'd been plenty of it.

Well, the Big Apple was history, wasn't it? No sense wishing for the unattainable. No sense chasing down a past that hadn't turned out the way it was supposed to.

Shake it off, Nadine.

Zach still hadn't moved, but his intensity snagged

her attention. What went on in the man's mind when he gazed about with such deep, earnest interest?

She reached the bottom stair. He stepped down and loomed over her. She was tall. He was taller. He smelled nice, like soap.

"Zach."

"Nadine."

She held out one hand to shake. He took it in his, calluses rubbing roughly against her palm, but released it when two kids, a pair of identical twins, came running out of the house.

She guessed them to be about seven years old, but what did she know? She didn't have a lot of exposure to children. They each carried a single rubber boot. Two different boots.

"I wanted to get just plain black," one boy shouted, "but Aiden wouldn't."

"The lady is pretty," the other boy said. Oh, sweet. "She might want flowers."

Zach grasped Nadine by the arms and spun her around.

"Oh!" *Whoa.*

"Sit," he said, "and we'll get you into those boots."

She sat on a step. He grasped her leg, not quite what she expected.

For a moment, he looked sheepish, as though he'd made a mistake. "Sorry. Didn't mean to be bossy. Can I take off your shoes?"

"Okay," she said. At her nod, he wrapped long fingers around one of her bare ankles to take off her shoe. Soda pop bubbles fizzed in her bloodstream. The twin who had called her pretty handed him a yellow boot with turquoise flowers on it. When Zach squatted on his haunches in front of Nadine, his face hovered close enough for her to detect flecks of yellow in his hazel eyes.

One of the boys, the flower boot one, distracted her by staring at her pink toenails. He grinned and said, "Nice color."

Nadine didn't know how to react. The only children she'd spent any time with were her friends' kids—the kids they insisted on having as they married and started families.

Zach gripped Nadine's other ankle in his warm hand and pulled off her second shoe. The soda pop bubbles went electric.

Double whoa. Heat suffused her.

"Can I sit here?" The first boy cuddled close to her on the step. The second boy copied him on her other side. Like a pair of bookends, they nestled against her.

These males overwhelmed her, even the young ones. "Sure you can sit," she said. "It's your house. But—"

Zach finished sliding the black boot onto her other foot and stood up. He stepped away with a satisfied smile on his face. Worn jeans hung low on his narrow hips. Biceps filled out his white T-shirt.

"There," he said. "Now you're ready for walking on the ranch. Can't walk it in high heels."

Nadine stared at the mismatched boots on her feet, the flowered one spotless. Straw and muck clung to the dark one. Oh, God, she hoped it was only muck. The rubber boots mocked all the care she'd taken with her choice of dress and the meticulous application of her makeup this morning.

She might no longer work in New York, but she maintained standards.

Glancing up at Zach, she said, "I brought a pair of boots. They're in the car."

He stared at her. "Really? I—" A blush crept up his neck, darkening the tanned skin and spreading into his cheeks. "You did?" Wonder of wonders, the guy looked awkward and not at all his usual assured self. She'd never seen him less than together before.

It kind of charmed her.

She bit back a smile. "Yes. You said we'd be walking so I came prepared."

"Oh…" He rubbed the back of his neck. "I thought you'd forgotten."

Was he as shy as he looked? *Shy* wasn't a word Nadine had ever applied to Zach Brandt. Intense, quiet, self-contained, certain of his place in the world, yes. But shy? No.

Also, masculine. *Let's not forget that, Nadine.*

"Do you want to change into your own boots?" he asked.

"Perhaps after we do the first part of the interview," she said.

"The first part?"

"Yes. I hoped to see your studio. Maybe take a look at your current work." She wanted to ease into that other story. Lee's story. The *real* one, he'd said. The longer she could put off Lee's agenda, the better.

Her stomach threatened to send up her breakfast. Wouldn't *that* be the epitome of embarrassing?

If she could concentrate on Zach's paintings first, maybe it would become possible to segue into questions about his family's past. Her problem lay in how to ask those uncomfortable questions.

"No," Zach said and he didn't look happy.

"No?" Immersed in her own troubling thoughts, she'd lost track of the conversation.

"This interview is not about my paintings alone. There are no paintings without the land."

"Yes, we'll cover everything. But your painting is a big part of who you are."

"This ranch—" he flung an arm toward the fields "—is a big part of who I am. That's what the readers will relate to. The land, not paintings."

Nadine could have argued that point, but too much of her energy today had been taken up by the conversation she'd had with her boss just before driving here. She should ignore it and try to forget, just do her job as she should, but that one misbegotten discussion had rocked her world in the worst possible way.

Pushing up her metaphorical sleeves, she opened her mouth to get this show on the road, but Zach pointed behind her.

"You know my dad, Rick Brandt."

She turned around on the step to peer up. Nadine smiled. She liked Rick and the perpetual twinkle in his eyes. Where Zach was reserved, his father was gregarious and friendly. Where Zach was long and muscular, Rick was short and spare.

"These are my boys, Ryan and Aiden." Zach gestured toward the twins, pointing to each one as he said his name. No way would Nadine be able to tell them apart.

They were vaguely familiar to her. She'd probably seen them around town, of course, but hadn't paid them much attention. Kids weren't on her radar, probably because there weren't stories attached to them. She could talk to anyone on any subject, but foreign little creatures called children stumped her. She liked kids, in theory. She just didn't know what to say to them, or how to entertain them.

Judging by expressions as watchful as their father's,

she didn't think the twins would go in for fist bumps, or that lamest of lame adult gestures—high fives.

So she smiled, wiggled her fingers hello and turned her attention back to Zach.

"I thought we could start with a look at your studio while you tell me about your inspiration. I have a list of questions for you. Things like when did you start painting, how young were you when you realized you had talent, did you—?"

"Dad," Zach interrupted, directing his attention to Rick, "we'll be gone for a while. Can you have lunch ready in an hour and a half?"

Nadine stared. People did *not* interrupt her so rudely.

Rick grinned and said, "Sure thing. Come on back when you're done and I'll have food on the table."

Zach nodded and strode away toward an outbuilding without another word for her.

Rick said, "You'd better hurry and join him or you'll have to run to catch up. Zach waits for nobody." He herded the boys into the house, leaving Nadine alone to stare at Zachary Brandt's retreating back.

She was not, and never had been, *nobody*. Certain people had tried to make her believe so, but she'd fought back. Oh, how she had fought. And she'd won. For a while.

Nadine Campbell was *somebody*, even if she had hit a bump in the road recently.

She crossed her arms and waited to see how long it would take Zach to realize she wasn't following like a meek little lamb. But when he entered the barn, he didn't turn back to check her progress.

Five minutes later, he still hadn't come out.

It seemed to her that he didn't much care whether she

followed. She didn't like the way *he* planned to conduct *her* interview.

She could leave. She wanted to.

Who was she kidding? After the things Lee had said this morning, Nadine was trapped here until she got the full story that Lee wanted. It was either that or lose her job, which she could *not* afford to do.

She picked up her high heels and carried them to the car, one boot too big and clunking as she crossed the hard-packed earth of the driveway. She set her shoes side by side neatly on the floor mat behind the driver's seat. For a moment, she considered changing into her own boots, but glanced back at the house. There in the middle of a big picture window were two small figures watching her.

If she changed out of the boots the boys had brought her, she might hurt their feelings. So she didn't.

Folding her arms, she leaned back against the car. Still no sign of Zach coming back out of the stable.

This morning's meeting with Lee ran through her mind again. If she could, if it were the least bit possible, she would have quit on the spot, not only because of the orders he gave her, but most especially because of his tone. She'd gone down to the office only to pick up a notebook she'd left on her desk. Lee had ambushed her.

"I was talking to my mother yesterday at the nursing home," he'd said apropos of nothing, seated at his desk and not looking up from his computer.

With a patience often needed in conversations with her boss, she waited out the ensuing silence.

He finished checking his email and said, "She told me some interesting things about the Brandt family. Some intriguing history."

"Such as?"

"Such as a big secret the family has never disclosed." He left it at that and stared at her.

What did that have to do with her and the interview? "And?"

"And *you* have to find out what that secret is."

"Why?"

"Because I want to know. If it's super juicy, the rest of the town will want to know, too."

"But why would it be anyone's business but the family's? Everyone in town respects them."

"Not everyone."

Nadine cocked her head and Lee continued, "There's been no love lost between them and their neighbors for a long time."

Their neighbors were the Broomes. Nadine remembered Tommy Broome from high school. Like Zach, he'd been two years ahead of her. Her memories of him weren't all good. He'd been aggressive. A bit of a bully.

"There's a rivalry between them, that's for sure," Lee said.

"Why? About what?"

"A feud of some sort."

"A *feud*? That's implies more than a rivalry."

"Yep."

"What was the source of the rivalry?"

"Don't honestly know. Usually these kinds of fights start because of one of three things." He ticked them off on his fingers. "Greed. Love. Sex."

"What does that have to do with Zach's paintings?"

Lee shrugged. "Nothing."

And then she knew. "You used the excuse of Zach's artistic abilities to get me out on that ranch to interview him."

"Yep." That one word, unapologetic, fueled Nadine's

anger. It had been Lee who had urged her to write an article about the Cowboy Painter.

When had Lee changed so much from when she'd worked for him in high school? And why? He didn't used to be...nasty.

"You used me," she said, betrayal scooting along her nerves.

"Yep." Lee threaded his fingers together across his stomach and leaned back in his chair. He didn't used to be smug, either. "You need to find out what the old secret is."

"How on earth am I supposed to do that?"

"That's your problem. You're the reporter." Lee's tone, a mix between order and dismissal, was exactly the problem with working for him.

"Can you give me a hint?" she asked. "What's the secret about?"

"My mom's being coy. Said she'll only talk to Zach about it. It's going to be your job to get him out to her nursing home."

"Why don't you just phone him and talk to him?"

Lee turned away. "We don't exactly get along."

See, this was where Nadine and Lee differed. Sure, she was a reporter and liked scoping out stories, but she wasn't a gossip. She often missed the more salacious stuff going on around town because she wasn't interested. Rumors and titillation didn't appeal to her. The truth did.

"Why don't you and Zach get along?" she asked, because even if this devolved into gossip, it seemed it would have something to do with her getting a story about Zach.

"We had a run-in a couple of years ago."

"About what?"

"It doesn't matter." For a man who usually talked

about anything and everything, Lee was being awfully cagey.

Nadine was twenty-nine, which meant Zach must be thirty-one and Lee past retirement age at well over sixty. So whatever the fallout was about, Zach and Lee likely weren't fighting about a woman. As far as Nadine knew, they had no business dealings, so it wasn't about money.

What was it? Lee wasn't talking.

"I can't butt into the Brandts' decades-old history," Nadine said. "I'm going out there to talk to Zach about his artwork."

Her hand was already on the doorknob when Lee said, "You ignore what I want and you're fired."

Her breath caught in her throat. "What?" *Fired?* Disappointment followed yet another burst of betrayal.

Had she done something wrong in the past year of working for Lee? Something that had upset him? Nothing she could think of.

"I'm giving you a job to do and by God, you'll do it." Lee stood, all five feet six inches, hundred and fifty pounds of him bristling like a hedgehog. "Weasel that secret out of Zach. I don't care how. Just do it."

He was, as it turned out, absolutely adamant. Nothing she had said after that had made a dent in his intention. It was either get the dirt or lose her job.

She needed her job, probably more than Lee even guessed. She'd left the office fuming. Now here she was on Zach's ranch with a chip on her shoulder and about as far from the top of her game as she could get.

She watched the barn. Not a sign of life there. The man wasn't coming back for her and she couldn't leave. Head down, she trudged forward.

Nadine Campbell, you've met your match.

Chapter Two

Zach stood in his stable and let the cool, soothing darkness wash the heat of embarrassment from his cheeks. He'd made a fool of himself lunging at Nadine to make her sit for those damned boots.

Smooth, Zach.

His campaign hadn't started well. He was better than this. Experienced with women. Not awkward and— lunge-y? *Damn it, Brandt, you screwed up already.*

He should have known she'd bring her own boots. She might be fashionable and perfectly turned out every day, but she was smart. She wouldn't walk his fields in high heels.

How long would it take her to follow him in? He grinned. On the one hand, she'd pestered him for an interview about his painting, clearly motivated to be here. On the other hand, he knew she was proud. She might drive off in an indignant huff. He wouldn't blame her. He liked that feisty part of Nadine and wanted to see her riled—anything other than the neutral, blank expression she wore too often since coming home.

He also admired her boundless curiosity, except when she applied it to him. He didn't want to do this interview. He wasn't comfortable talking about himself. Never had been.

He wasn't verbal. His paintings said all there was to say about him.

So why had he given in to her? To get her out on his ranch once more. *Zach Brandt, you are so pathetic.*

Again, he grinned. Pathetic, yeah, but also smart like a fox. If he had to submit to being interviewed, so be it. He hadn't pursued her back in high school because he'd known she had ambitions and would leave town for good eventually. For some reason, she'd come back home. She was free. As far as he knew, and he'd asked around, she had no significant other in her life. He was available since his divorce three years ago.

But what would this new adult Nadine think of his ranch? Would she like it any better than she had when she was younger?

There was no point in asking a woman out on a date if she hated what you did for a living.

Where was she?

She had her pride, and he wasn't going back outside to get her. Her curiosity would get the better of her. Any minute now, she would give in and come to get him.

By the time he'd greeted all of his horses with nose rubs and baby carrots from his shirt pocket, she still hadn't shown up. She was tougher than he'd thought. Still biding his time, he stepped into the back room that was his studio in the summer months.

Spotless, the room welcomed him like a long-lost buddy, the smell of paint as familiar here as hay, manure, dust motes and horses.

He stared at the canvas sitting on the easel, an unfinished landscape that had been giving him fits. It was a study of his mountain at sunset, and he hadn't yet gotten the red right where the light reflected on the tip. He mixed too bright or too dull, too orange or too blue.

An old enemy—frustration in his lack of ability—ate
at him. Buyers might praise his talent, but he knew better. He knew how far he missed the mark of perfection.
He knew how arrogant he was to even try to reproduce
what Mother Nature had already presented with such
unadulterated splendor.

Still, he strove to interpret and produce his love of the
land. He couldn't stop painting if he tried. The canvas,
the paint, called to him.

There *had* to be a way to mix that particular red.
Maybe if he tried adding a little…

With the flash of an idea that just might work, he
picked up his palette and mixed. Close. Closer. When
he applied brush and paint to canvas, he lost track of
time. He lost himself.

Burdens, worries, conflicts fell away. All was peace.

NADINE WALKED TO the barn with slow steps, the too-large
boot hitting the ground with a thunk every time. Funny
how much guilt weighed. Tons.

Find out that family's secrets.

The inside of the barn was empty save for a few
horses. Maybe Zach had fooled her and left by a back
door. But why would he? He'd agreed to the interview.
She hadn't forced it on him.

Where had he gone?

A faint sound reached her from the back of the building. She followed it to an ancient wooden door standing ajar with sunlight streaming through the gap. She
peeked inside.

Zach stood in front of an easel, painting. He'd *forgotten* about her! Nadine didn't have a huge ego, but people
didn't tend to forget her. Her looks alone had garnered

all kinds of attention in the city. Well, her new, refined looks had.

It had taken a massive makeover to even be considered by a TV station. And finally, one had hired her. She had mattered then, to her bosses and to her audience.

Apparently, she didn't mean much to Zach. Or perhaps, to be realistic, his painting mattered more.

Why should she be important to him? She was just a girl he'd gone to school with. Not even that. Two years younger than him, she hadn't shared classes with him. He probably hadn't even noticed her back then.

He painted with his whole body. Considering he held himself still except for the brush in his hand stroking red paint onto a mountaintop, she wasn't sure what she meant by that. Understanding came quickly. Zach's passion for painting was so deeply ingrained, his brush was being wielded by his soul.

Was there anything in Nadine's life to compare?

Yes. Her writing. When she was involved in a story, she forgot everything else around her. Now, because of her boss, that process had been tainted. Lee had turned it into a distasteful job.

A ray of sunshine poured from a small high window onto Zach's head like a benediction. Like the hand of God. And here she was, an instrument of either a very unkind god, or the devil, to destroy him.

Hyperbole, Nadine. Yeah, but knowing the little bit she did about the man and his character, this story might very well destroy him. What secrets could there be in his family's past?

Lee had intimated that there was a huge, ugly, *significant* secret. Nadine couldn't imagine that and had told him so.

Oh, yes, Lee had countered, secrets abounded on

this ranch, but the townspeople had never gotten the full story. That was her job. The Brandts were, and always had been, respected in Rodeo. They were known throughout the state. Hadn't Zach's grandfather run for governor at one point? She had a lot of research ahead of her. And a lot of dirty delving.

Nadine watched Zach while he painted and found it magical.

Even in high school, she'd sensed he was a person of great integrity. As far as she knew, Zach had lived a good, blameless life in his first thirty-one years. Whatever Lee thought had happened in this family must be big, or he wouldn't be so fixated on her getting the info. Which meant that when it got out, it could very well damage this family.

Nadine had to bring down an honest man.

Arising out of a misty internal landscape, Zach became aware of his surroundings…and of the paintbrush in his hand he'd barely realized he'd picked up. That's how it was with his painting, captivating him in unguarded moments.

His skin prickled. Someone was watching him. He glanced to his right.

Standing in the doorway, leaning against the frame with her arms crossed, stood Nadine. He'd forgotten about her, not an easy feat considering her vibrant beauty and strong personality. Or what used to be a strong personality. Something had happened to her in the city. Something had dampened her enthusiasm.

Zach wanted to know what that was.

One rubber-booted foot rested across the other, out of harmony with the deep green dress wrapped across her flat stomach and tied in a discreet bow at the side, that small flare the only spot of decoration on the garment.

The finely tailored dress outlined her figure without showing too much, tasteful while still displaying trim assets. She must lift weights or work out, he guessed, because her biceps looked strong. So did her calves. But then, he'd already felt how fit her legs were when he'd put the boots on her feet.

Inside of those boots, he knew, were pink toenails to nearly match her pink fingernails. A connoisseur of color, he'd already noted that they were two different shades of pink. As though her body were a canvas, Nadine took the time to choose different colors for her feet and hands.

His gaze caressed high cheekbones and a strong jaw. How difficult would her face be to paint? Being easy on the eye didn't always translate onto the canvas.

The green of the dress did amazing things to her green eyes. Shadows hovered in those eyes. She had been private back in high school, but now she was downright shuttered. Locked up tight.

Nadine had been hiding inside of herself since coming home. How he knew that when he'd barely had contact with her in that time was hard to say, but he observed, constantly, everyone and everything around him. He would love to breach her defenses to learn the woman beneath her sophisticated exterior. With an artist's sensibilities, he knew her beauty was more than skin-deep, but why did she hide what was inside of her?

What drove her extreme need for privacy?

She watched him steadily but without anger at being abandoned, as far as he could tell.

"How long?" he asked.

She understood him right away, glancing at her watch,

a tiny bit of filigreed gold on her left wrist. Could it even be called a watch?

"Forty minutes."

Forty minutes!

Zach wasn't prone to blushing, but heat traveled up his chest and into his cheeks for the second time that morning. He hadn't meant to be rude. Well, not *this* rude. Nor did he like people watching him while he painted.

The act of painting was a deeply private enterprise for him. He made only the finished product available for public consumption. But he had, in effect, invited her to look for him back here by abandoning her in the yard and expecting her to follow him to the stable.

Then he'd forgotten himself enough to start to paint. What would she write about it?

Funny, the guy seemed to go into a trance while he left me waiting to interview him. Rudeness must be Zachary Brandt's middle name.

Would Nadine say things like that about him? Maybe. Maybe not. He might think he knew her, but what he knew was an old version of her. *That* Nadine might well be obsolete by now.

She didn't look put out. She looked curious, avidly drinking in the details of the room. She stepped forward and studied the work in progress while Zach held his breath.

Though his paintings might be so personal that he didn't care what people thought of them, Nadine's opinion mattered.

"It's magnificent," she said, and he believed she meant it. She wasn't just buttering him up to get a better article out of him.

The warm feelings flooding his veins disconcerted

him. He stood abruptly. "Let's go," he said and left his studio, judging that she'd follow him this time.

In the larger room with the horses, he asked, "Do you ride?"

"Yes. Why?"

"We could ride out on the land while we talk."

"You mean, while you talk and I listen. This is an interview, Zack, not a conversation."

He glanced at her dress. "I guess we won't be riding today unless you want to borrow some of my clothes."

"They wouldn't fit."

"Why did you come out to a ranch dressed like that?"

"Because I'm here as a professional."

"Wouldn't a professional dress appropriately for the situation?"

By the displeasure on her face, he knew his barb had hit home.

"You wanted to avoid getting out on the land, didn't you? Why?"

ZACH SCARED NADINE.

No, that wasn't quite right. He intimidated her. He saw too much. His question was fair.

He had hit the nail on the head, exposing and smashing the arguments she'd used for why she hadn't worn pants and a simple shirt today. A pro would dress for the situation and the terrain. She had tried to keep control of the interview by not wearing practical clothing.

She'd thought she could get away with photographing him and interviewing him only in his studio by wearing a dress. The boots she'd thrown into the trunk had been an afterthought.

That's not all, Nadine. As much as she knew her readers would love to know more about Zach, she didn't want to get anywhere near him. She'd worn her professional outfit as a shield.

The resounding answer to his question was—drumroll, please—that she wanted Zach to see her only one way: as a professional and not as a woman.

Given what she was about to put him through in the course of writing this article, she didn't welcome her attraction to him. She wouldn't welcome his attraction to her. If there was any. She thought there used to be, but that was a long time ago, in a different life.

In New York City, she'd learned a lot about makeup and good clothing and putting her best foot forward. Plenty of men had found her attractive. The men of New York liked this version of her.

But Zach…it was like he saw through her and that unsettled her, even as she reasoned that there was nothing to *see through*. In New York, she had simply learned to be a far, far better version of herself. Her thoughts, her emotions, her justifications for any and all decisions in her life were hers and hers alone. They were none of his business.

Still, he waited with that unnerving stare.

Let's keep things light and on the surface, she thought.

On the other hand, wasn't she here to get to know him better? Wasn't the point of her interview to find out as much as she could about the man?

Zach had never been the kind of person to give much of himself away. Even in high school, he'd been intensely private. And though they'd grown up in the same town, and they both lived here now, he remained a mystery.

Who was Zach Brandt?

Oh, well, what she couldn't get from him, she would get from others. She would talk to his buddies in town. She would interview his father.

Nadine always got her story.

"Okay, we can't ride today," Zach said, ignoring the fact that she hadn't answered his question about going out on the land. "We'll go for a walk."

He obviously assumed she would do anything he wanted.

"You didn't dress for riding," he continued, "but you will the next time you come out."

The next time? Yes, of course, there would be a next time. She couldn't get everything she needed in one visit. If only she could and then never have to face Zach again.

Detach, Nadine. Detach.

While maintaining objectivity might be a normal part of journalism, it had never felt more important than today. She built her barriers brick by brick.

"Do you ride well?" he asked.

"Not well, but I can ride enough to see some of the land."

"Okay, one of the things we'll do in this whole inter-view process is to get out there together on horseback."

"Do we have to? Why can't we just talk?"

A corner of Zach's mouth kicked up. "Do I seem like much of a talker to you?"

A laugh burst out of her. "No."

"Exactly."

She liked this self-aware joking side of the man.

One by one, Zach led his horses out of the stable and into a corral along the side of the building. Nadine fol-lowed him out of the barn to watch them prance in the sun. Thank goodness it wasn't raining. She felt more comfortable with Zach in the outdoors than in a con-fined space like the stable, and especially that small studio, even if it was best to do the interview there and concentrate only on his artwork. The man was too big and too warm.

He stood with the easy, loose-hipped grace of a man comfortable in his own body. And what a body it was—lean but strong, and muscled in all the right places. His dark hair curled over his collar. It had fallen forward across his forehead while he painted.

She'd caught a rare glimpse of an unguarded moment. He'd been focused and contained and lost somewhere deep inside. Still waters had never run so deeply.

She opened the bag slung over her shoulder and pulled out her small voice recorder. "I have to warn you that I'm going to record the interview."

He frowned at the device, eyes piercing.

"What's wrong?" she asked. Did he think she had a perfect memory? All journalists used some kind of recording method.

He kept staring at it.

"I can't remember everything and it's hard to take notes out here. May I record or not?" What an odd thing for him to object to. Maybe he didn't like the actual formality of an interview. Maybe he was more comfortable just talking. Some subjects were like that.

He took his time, but eventually Zach shrugged and said, "Okay."

She pressed Record. "When did you first realize you wanted to paint? And how did you get started?"

He turned to stare at his horses and settled the black cowboy hat in his hand onto his head. "I can't remember how old I was when I first started to draw. I assume I was very young or I would remember. Maybe my father can tell you more about that."

"I'll ask him." She waited, but he said nothing more. "And *how* did you start?" she prompted.

"I assume with crayons." A hint of sarcasm colored his tone.

"Don't you know? What did your parents tell you?"

"Nothing. I've never asked. I don't know how my artistic drive started because it has just always been part of me."

"It sounds like I'll get more information out of your father than out of you."

He smiled. "In that area, yeah." He pushed away from the fence. "Let's walk."

Nadine hitched her bag higher onto her shoulder.

Zach took it from her and said, "We can come back for this."

"But—"

"Isn't the tape recorder enough?"

She studied it. Why did she need anything else right now? "Yes. I guess it is."

Zach hung her bag from a fencepost and started to amble along the side of the corral.

Her wistful glance lingered on her bag. She didn't need it at the moment, but this interview seemed to be moving out of her control. But that wasn't Zach's fault, really, was it? Lee had done that to her. He'd rattled her.

Struggling to regain some semblance of her identity as a reporter, she asked, "What motivates you, Zach?"

He swept his arm wide. "This is it—all the motivation I need."

They rounded the back of the stable and started into a field. Nadine pointed to the low mountain in the distance. "I recognize that. That's what you were working on in the studio."

He nodded. "My favorite part of the ranch. The view from the top is spectacular. We'll head up there at some point. You need to see it to understand my paintings."

She stumbled and he caught her elbow. "Okay?"

When she was steady, she shied away from his firm touch. "I blame the mismatched boots."

He frowned. "Do you want to go back for yours?"

She shook her head. "I'll be fine. What do you see when you look at your land?"

"I imagine the same thing you do. Maybe my brain interprets it differently, that's all."

She stopped. "You aren't giving me much."

He held up his hands, palms out. "What do you want me to say? I see the land. I paint it. It's that simple."

Nadine struggled to rein in her frustration. Maybe she wasn't asking the right questions. "But where does the depth come from?"

"From a love of the land."

If he didn't give her more than one-sentence answers and circular explanations, she wasn't going to end up with much of an article. She glanced around.

"Tell me," he said. "What do you see?"

"A pretty landscape, but what I see doesn't matter, does it? This article will be about you. How does the vision for your paintings develop?"

"It doesn't develop. It just is."

"Do you mean you see the world differently than other people do?"

"Differently than you do, that's for certain," he said under his breath. "When I'm out on my own, I'm aware of every little thing. I can't be articulate and poetic about the land. Words aren't my forte. Painting is. So how can I describe the process to you when there isn't one, when what you see on my canvasses is the answer to all of your questions?"

She frowned. At least he was talking more. "I can't

write an article on so flimsy an account. I can't just publish photographs of your work."

"Why not?"

"Because the public wants to know who *you* are, the man behind the paintings."

"Everyone in Rodeo already knows who I am."

"The *Rodeo Wrangler*'s readership spreads through the entire county. You know that."

"They don't need me to explain my paintings to them."

"That's my job. I can explain that to them."

"I doubt it. You don't know me from Adam."

She choked out a sound of frustration. "That's why I'm here today. To get to know you better."

He didn't respond.

"Okay," she said. "I'll tell you what I saw while you were painting." She sensed Zach becoming still beside her, but she pushed on. "I saw such intensity. You don't seem like an emotional man, but I sensed an emotional connection to the land."

"Yeah, I guess."

"But it's also a spiritual connection, I think. You looked…at peace, Zach."

If she sounded a little envious, it was because she felt that way. How did a person find that connection to the world? How did a person find where they belonged?

In New York City, Nadine. Remember?

Nope. Not anymore. She brushed aside the sadness that thought brought on, ruthless in her need to deny and forget.

Her stomach rumbled. She had a bad habit of skipping breakfast before heading out to interview or write an article. This morning had been no different.

Zach heard and steered them back toward the house.

"Sorry about the painting. I took so long we're going to miss some of today's interview time. Dad will have lunch ready by now."

"But I need more, Zach."

"I understand. You'll get more. You're coming back tomorrow to ride, remember?"

He grinned and she swore her heartbeat stuttered.

But she wanted this all settled quickly. As much as she wanted to avoid Lee's angle, she couldn't. Only when it was written and published could she move forward. One more life destroyed. But it was the price she had to pay if she wanted her life back. Wasn't it?

Oh, God.

Her fingers tingled with the need to learn the awful secret and type up everything, finish the article and then crawl into bed to hide from the fallout that was sure to follow. How had her life become so screwed up?

They entered the house together. Zach toed off his cowboy boots while Nadine left the rubber boots he'd given her neatly on a mat.

"Lunch is ready," his father called from the back of the house.

Zach led her to the kitchen where the two boys already waited at a large wooden table. Three other places had been set. Zach pulled out a chair for her and she sat.

While Zach and Rick served canned tomato soup and basic grilled cheese sandwiches, Nadine thought back to some of the amazing sandwiches she'd had in New York City with all of its different restaurants and cuisines. This didn't begin to compare.

Zach sat down and met her eye. Had he guessed what she was thinking? She should be careful that she didn't let that kind of attitude bleed through. Why should she compare the two? Rodeo, Montana, was valid in its own right. She'd been raised on canned soup and white bread sandwiches, even if her tastes had changed.

Fortunately these days, she could indulge her new tastes at the Summertime Diner. Violet Summer did an amazing job of elevating old classics.

Who knew? Someday Nadine might be working for Vy. If Nadine couldn't get the information Lee wanted, she could kiss her career goodbye, a thought that pained her deep in her soul. She probably would end up working as a waitress for Vy.

Not that there was anything wrong with the job, but it wouldn't fill her passion for reporting, interviewing and writing, would it?

She wasn't meant to do anything other than report on people, places and things. Journalism had saved her life. It had made her adolescence bearable. It had made life with her aunt less devastating.

How could she give it up now? Writing was her only purpose in life. Her passion. Without it, she would be aimless and lost.

A part of her would die.

Throughout the quiet, uncomfortable meal, the children stared at her. Her smiles for them, while genuine, were restrained. She just didn't know what to *do* with children. How should she talk to them? What should she say?

In high school, while other kids were earning money babysitting, she had been writing articles for the high school newsletter and for the *Rodeo Wrangler*.

She was more comfortable with her friends' children, maybe because they were little pieces of her friends in miniature form. She wasn't comfortable with Zach, so perhaps there was a double whammy thing happening here. She couldn't relax around Zach. It made sense she couldn't relax around his children, either.

After what felt like an eternity, Nadine put down her spoon, her soup bowl empty. It might have been plain food, but it brought back memories of lunch in the high school cafeteria with her friends, and that wasn't a bad thing. She wondered if they were still serving the same food or if they'd updated it by now. Teenagers were a lot savvier than they used to be.

Funny, she'd enjoyed the soup and sandwich after all.

If only the children would stop sneaking peeks at her. She wanted to ask Rick questions about Zach, but would rather not do it in front of the children. Instead, she engaged him in chatter about things going on around town.

Eventually, one of the boys—Ryan, maybe?—piped up.

"You write?" he asked. He'd been fidgeting throughout lunch.

"Yes. I write articles for the *Rodeo Wrangler* about all the things that go on around town." She cursed the sound of her voice, too fake and hearty. Even to her own ears, it betrayed her unease with the little boys.

The child fixed her with an intent gaze. "Can you read my story?"

"You wrote something?" she asked. "How wonderful." She, too, had written stories at that age.

He nodded. "Can you read it?"

"I guess that would be all right."

"Great."

He got up from the table, but Zach said, "Aiden," in a quiet but firm voice.

Aiden stopped and looked at his father.

"After dessert."

"Okay, Dad." Aiden sat back down.

Obedient kids.

Throughout a long dessert—long to Nadine, at any rate, with Zach quiet and intense at the opposite end of the table and the two boys fidgeting until the last mouthful was swallowed—she tried to relax.

Was that what children did, fidgeted, or were these two unusually active? Zach didn't seem to notice or mind.

When he stood, Nadine breathed relief. His father collected dirty plates and cutlery. When Nadine offered to wash dishes, he waved her away. "Go read Aiden's story."

Zach led her to the living room and motioned for her to sit on the sofa. Aiden and Ryan ran into the room and jumped up beside her, nestling as close as they could on either side.

"Oh!" She wasn't used to children crowding her. Nadine tried to pull away, but there was nowhere to go, bracketed as she was by the boys. She allowed Aiden to insert his head up under her arm so she had no choice but to put her arm around him.

Friendly little guy. His twin did the same on the other side.

Aiden retrieved something from the small table beside the sofa.

"Here." He thrust a folder at her, homemade from yellow Bristol board and decorated with a drawing of a boy on a horse. She smiled, wondering if he wanted to be a painter like his dad one day.

She took her arm from around Ryan's shoulder and gingerly accepted the story from Aiden, avoiding the small blob of cheese still stuck to one of his fingers. Her dress had been expensive when she'd bought it three years ago. She couldn't afford to replace it if grease from that cheese stained it.

Go clean your hands. Where do you think we live? In a barn?

Nadine shut out that voice so she could give Aiden's story her full attention. She opened the folder. Large, childish printing covered four sheets of lined paper, front and back.

"Read it out loud," Aiden ordered.

With the boys' warm weight tucked close to her sides, she read Aiden's story…and was charmed. The story of what he knew—life on a ranch—delighted her.

When she closed the folder, he leaned forward and twisted around until he could look up at her. "Is it good?"

"Yes, it is." How could she deny that earnest gaze anything? "It's a *wonderful* story."

His smile warmed her heart. "What was the best part?" he asked.

"When the boy rescued the pony from the crevasse he'd fallen into."

"Yeah! That's my favorite part, too. Boys are good at rescuing."

"Girls, too," Nadine said, but Aiden's returning look was dubious.

Oh, dear. She shot a glance at Zach who said, "Girls, too."

"Dad, tell her," Ryan ordered. "Boys do the rescuing. Not girls."

"Son, this is a conversation we need to have later." His eyes met Nadine's. "And we will."

His promise eased her concerns. "Girls can be anything they want to be," Nadine said.

"Anything?" Aiden asked.

"Anything."

The earnest, matching expressions on the twin's faces were reminiscent of their dad's even if their eyes were a lot darker than his. Their mother's, perhaps?

She'd never met Zach's ex. Had never even seen her.

Aiden touched Nadine's chin to bring her attention back to him. She wondered whether the presence of a woman was unusual enough for them to vie for her attention.

"Tell me what else you liked," he said.

She outlined all that she thought was strong about his writing. Aiden watched her without a word, his serious attention charming her.

When she finished, he asked, "Can you put it in the paper?"

"The newspaper?"

"Yeah."

He'd surprised her. She had no idea what Lee would think. "I can ask the publisher, if you like."

He nodded so hard a hank of hair fell across his forehead. "I'll write another story," he said. "Just for you!"

Nadine looked at Ryan on her other side. "Do you write, too?"

"No, but look what I can do!"

He jumped up from the sofa and did a somersault across the carpet.

Aiden joined him and they started to roughhouse.

They rolled around on the floor like a pair of bear cubs in freshly fallen snow, so much like two halves of a whole it was hard to tell where one started and the other ended.

Zach and Rick carried on a conversation with Nadine, asking questions about how the fair was coming along— Nadine was on the Rodeo Revival committee, and the event was only a month away—while she kept her eye on the two boys grappling and giggling.

Apparently, this was normal. Neither Zach nor Rick batted an eye. But Nadine noticed…and remembered the admonishments she'd received as a young preteen.

Don't slouch. Stand up straight.

Only speak when spoken to.

Don't get your clothes dirty.

Put your books away now. Cleanliness is next to godliness.

Tidy up. Tidy up. Tidy up.

Do better.

Brush out those ridiculous curls.

Be a good girl.

And the worst of all: *You're just like your mother.*

Considering that she'd always adored her mother, Nadine hadn't understood what her aunt meant by that. Not when she'd first arrived in town as an eleven-year-old, at least. But in time, her aunt had made certain Nadine was clear that it wasn't a compliment.

The loop of recriminations hadn't stopped, even with her aunt's death four years ago. Like a Möbius strip that never ended, Nadine had internalized her aunt's voice.

God, she was tired of it.

The twins stopped fighting and ran from the room. They pounded up the stairs. Nadine meant to get her story as quickly and painlessly as possible and then stay far, far away from Zachary Brandt and his enchanting boys.

Chapter Three

Nadine parked her car on Main Street, wishing for the hundredth time that she had a garage to protect it from the elements. She needed a car in rural Montana, but if something serious happened to the one she had, she wouldn't have money for another unless her circumstances changed drastically.

She hadn't saved money in New York. She might have worked long hours, but living there was expensive.

Lee didn't pay her well. If she didn't get this story and he fired her, getting another job in her field would be nearly impossible after that incident in New York.

She couldn't think about it. Couldn't face her own hubris. Had left it behind in the Big Apple.

Her stomach cramped. She picked up her bag and walked down Main to the *Rodeo Wrangler* office, staring at the gold and black lettering on the door.

Lee had made promises when she'd come home.

He had no children. No heirs. He'd intimated he wanted to retire. He needed someone to take over.

That someone would be her.

Coming home in a state of utter loss, his promise had been a prayer answered.

But now she faced this changed man and his unreasonable demand.

Lee stood in the large plate glass window watching her approach.

When she'd worked for him in high school, she had never gotten a bad feeling from Lee. He'd given her a first shot at journalism and she had been grateful. Who was this man he'd become and what had he done with the Lee Beeton she'd known?

Despite her anger and feelings of betrayal, sadness filled her.

He'd once been a decent man.

Judging by the look in his eye, he was in the same mood as when she'd left to go out to the Brandt ranch. He would want a full report, she was sure. His gaze seemed almost malevolent.

Boy, she was chock-full of exaggeration today. Or maybe not.

How could she have misjudged him so badly? As a teenager, she had thanked him profusely for the oppor-tunities and the experience. And when she'd returned to Rodeo a year ago with her tail between her legs, Lee had once again agreed to give her a job. She'd seen signs that he had changed. Grouchiness. Tension. Impatience. Her friends had said he'd been slowly becoming more bad-tempered over the years. Nadine had ignored all of this, but could no longer.

Not with his demand for dirt on a fellow citizen.

She stepped into the office.

Without preamble, he asked, "Did you get it?"

"The story? Of course not, Lee. That was just the first interview. I can't jump into the nitty-gritty without gain-ing his trust first."

"Trust. Yeah. I guess so."

He *guessed* so? Lee knew how to conduct an inter-view and how to handle a subject. He'd been a good journalist in his time, but these days he seemed desperate. What was going on with him?

"Lee, if your mother has a memory of something fishy in the Brandt family, why don't you just ask her about it? Why send me to do your dirty work?"

"Because she isn't telling me. She said she needs to talk to Richard Brandt."

"Rick? Zach's father?"

"No. Richard—Zach's grandfather."

Dread settled into Nadine's stomach. "His grandfather who's been dead for decades? Does your mother not understand that he's gone?"

"Sometimes she's lucid and sometimes she isn't."

"So how can you trust anything she has to say? Maybe all her memories are suspect."

"Naw. When's she lucid, she'll remember the dress she wore on her first date and what they had for dinner that night."

"But that must have been one of the most significant nights of her life," Nadine ventured. "It makes sense she'd remember those details, but how can we trust that her memory of a secret about the Brandts is accurate, even if she tells you about it when she's lucid?"

"My mother and Zach's grandmother were best friends."

"I see."

Light through the window haloed Lee's head, the wisps of his remaining hair highlighted like cilia.

He wasn't taking care of himself these days. He used to be a nice-looking man with kind eyes, but he no longer seemed to care about his appearance. His old cardigan had a hole in it. A blob on his shirt that resembled Italy in the Rorschach test of food stains might have been made by spilled coffee. Some days, Nadine was certain he had forgotten to bathe.

Today wasn't one of those, thank goodness. The office wasn't large enough for her to avoid him when he smelled ripe.

At first she'd been concerned for his sake, for the loss of an old friend, but this morning he'd gone so far she was almost past caring. Almost.

On the drive back into town, she'd done a lot of thinking. "Why do you need me, Lee? Why not wait until your mom has a lucid moment and just listen to what she has to say about the past?"

Lee bristled. "I'm paying you good money to do a job, girl, and you'll do it."

Good money? Not by a long shot. And *girl*? What kind of way was that to speak to an employee? Lee didn't used to be rude.

"My mother won't confide in me. She rarely talks to me anymore. When she does, it's by accident." His gaze slid away from hers. "A year or so ago, we had a fight."

A falling-out with Zach. A fight with his mother. She remembered them as being close. "Why not wait until a day when maybe she's forgotten about that?"

"She's never forgiven me for the things I said." He added bitterly, "Her dementia has destroyed more memories than I've probably ever had in my lifetime, but she knows every word of that conversation by heart." He turned away from Main Street and said, "That's why I need you. She always liked you. She would talk to you."

"I'm not sure she would. You said first she would talk to only Zach and then only to Richard, his grandfather."

"Then get the secret from Zach," he snapped.

"Do you honestly think Zach will just give up a family secret that's so titillating you think it will sell extra issues of your paper?"

"No, he won't just *give it up*." Sarcasm. Another new feature with Lee. "Use your skills. Use whatever you have in your arsenal to get it out of him."

"But—"

"Where else do you think you could get a job in town? This is the only newspaper for miles around. If you want to continue to live in Rodeo and keep this job, then you'll do whatever you have to do to get me that article."

Something was making him desperate, and he was dead serious.

Sure, there were laws against this kind of workplace harassment and coercion, but she couldn't afford a lawyer.

He was right. If he fired her, she would have to move away from her friends to find another job in reporting. She'd come back home because of a mistake she had made, only one, but it had been a doozy.

She'd come back to the only home she knew, not because of the town or the geography, but because of her friends. They were her only family. Without them she was alone. That thought caused an ache so deep inside of her it felt like fire ate at her belly.

Her aunt had been her sole remaining blood relative. She had died four years ago and had decided to ignore Nadine in death. She'd left nothing to Nadine, not a single penny or knickknack, as though every speck of resentment she'd felt toward her niece had followed her into the afterlife.

So Nadine's family was Rachel, Violet, Honey and Max, all of them tied together by common experiences and similar heartbreaks. They were the town fair's Revival Committee, but also the best of friends, and now

Rachel's new sister-in-law, Samantha, had been added to the mix.

Nadine liked Rodeo. She liked the people here. She respected them.

Then Lee had told her the newspaper could be hers someday, a dream come true for her in Rodeo.

When she'd left town the first time, it had been her choice. She didn't want to be pushed out by someone else now, by Lee's need for a dirty article. Unfortunately, she couldn't live without the measly paycheck he paid her. Rodeo wasn't exactly a bustling town. Nadine wasn't even certain Vy could give her job at the diner, friend or not.

But even more important than losing a paycheck, she couldn't possibly lose her friendships. She'd lost a lot in New York City. Losing her friends would be far worse.

Nadine stared at her boss. "Lee, what's wrong?" She might be angry with him, but he had given her her first job and had encouraged her in her choice of career. He'd had enough faith in her skills to tell her that she could someday run this office. The small part of her that still cared worried about him.

"What's wrong?" she repeated.

He rubbed his stomach as though it ached. "Nothing."

Then he scrubbed his hands over his face. "I—I can't tell you."

He sounded more like the old Lee, as though he lurked inside of this new harder person.

"What can I do?" Nadine asked.

"Can you just get the story? Please?" Desperation again. "I meant what I said this morning, Nadine. Get me that story."

His tone might be softer and less mean, but the new

Lee was determined, leaving Nadine with no choice but to do what he wanted.

He glanced at her then away. "Take the afternoon off. Tomorrow will be soon enough to get back at it."

A peace offering, just when she was prepared to hate him.

She left and closed the door behind her.

When she stepped out onto Main Street, it looked the same as always…but also not. She'd gone through this before, in the city where her life had fallen apart. People walked down the street, smiling and waving as though life were normal. As though disaster, or the terrifying potential for it, hadn't rocked her world.

Her passion had always been journalism. It had given her an escape from loneliness and grief.

She'd lost New York City and that had been monumentally awful. This would be even worse. Rodeo was home. When she'd left NYC, she'd known she had Rodeo to fall back on. If she lost this job *and* Rodeo, she would have nothing.

If she got a job working for a newspaper in another small town, someplace desperate enough to hire her despite her mistake, she wouldn't have the warm cloak of her friendships to keep her sadness at bay.

Long-distance friendship had been okay while she had the excitement of her career in New York, but life in another small town without them close by would be unbearable.

She hadn't thought the bottom could fall out of her world again.

Nadine unlocked her door, trudged up the stairs to her apartment above the office and stepped into a neat, tidy, arid space that returned a bit of her calm to her. She hung her dress in the green section of her bedroom closet and took off her baby blue heels. She folded each shoe in the tissue paper from their box, then slid the box back into place. All of her nice clothes were leftovers from her career in New York, and she planned to make them last.

She'd only worn her dress for half the day. The next time she wore it, she would rinse it by hand. Like her car, she couldn't afford to replace her clothing. She didn't know what she would do once they wore out.

She could shop in thrift stores, or the consignment shop in the next town, but her beautiful clothes were the shield that blocked out the critical voice in her head that belonged to her aunt.

Consigning that worry to a far corner of her mind, she sat down to transcribe the recorded interview, only to realize how truly little she had wrung out of Zach. She tossed down her pen, glared around her spotless, well-ordered apartment and despaired.

For a whole year, she had avoided *feeling*. She'd lived a parched existence because it was the only life she could handle. Lee had forced her feelings, all of her high emotions, back to the forefront. She was being drawn back into life.

She didn't want this. She didn't want to feel.

She didn't want to remember.

The silence in the apartment resounded as though it had life and breath. She needed to get out of here.

Her phone rang. She grabbed it and checked the number. Violet. Thank God. When she answered, Nadine swallowed and forced herself to sound normal.

"What are you doing for supper?" Vy asked.

"Salad and tuna. Do you want to join me?"

"Thought you'd never ask. I'll be there at six."

Nadine spent the rest of the afternoon working on a couple of her regular columns, about events in the community, along with news about the townspeople that did not constitute gossip. She phoned around to get all of her facts straight. She sifted through her emails for announcements from people about the births, marriages and job promotions that filled her with pleasure, while deaths were few, thank goodness.

Vy arrived at six on the dot. Nadine rushed to her and gave her a big hug, holding on longer than she should have.

"Hey, hey, what's going on?" Vy pulled away, a searching look on her face.

"Lee's being an ass."

"He's been strange lately. What's going on with him?"

"I have no idea. He has these moods swings. At the moment, he's being strange and demanding."

"You said you were going out to Zach's farm today to interview him," Vy said. "How did that go?"

"Like pulling teeth."

"What did you expect? The guy's sociable, but private."

Private with a capital *P*.

Nadine prepared two servings of a salad and canned tuna with a sprinkling of lemon pepper. Vy nibbled on sliced radishes while Nadine worked.

"Hey." She swatted her friend's hand away. "There won't be any left for the salad."

"I'm starving."

"How can that be? You work in a diner."

"I'm pregnant, remember? I eat all the time these days."

"You're looking really good. You're glowing. I know it's a cliché, but it's true."

Vy grinned. The pregnancy might have been unplanned but all had worked out in the end, with the new stranger in town, Sam Carmichael, falling like a log for Vy and deciding to stay and marry her. How could he not? Vy was a great person.

Nadine returned the lemon pepper to the spice rack between the ground ginger and the mustard seed.

Vy set the table and they sat down to eat, discussing the upcoming revival of the renovated rodeo and fair. It had run for over a hundred years in Rodeo every summer without fail, until the owner retired fifteen years ago. He'd inherited it from his father, who had inherited it from his father.

His son had not been willing to carry on and the tradition had been broken.

Too many of the town's young were leaving. Nadine and her friends had decided it was time to do something about that, and they hoped the revival of the fair would be a viable solution for bringing in money and creating jobs.

Since no one else had managed to come up with solutions to help out their town, they'd taken it on.

This year, the fair would run for ten days spanning two weekends.

If it was a success, they could consider making it permanent and maybe even run it for longer in the coming years. Vy carried their dishes to the sink. "Sam's going to donate a couple of thousand dollars for you to use for more promotion."

Nadine stared at her friend. "Are you serious? That's fantastic."

Vy pulled a check out of her pocket and handed it over. "That's why I came over."

Nadine laughed. "But you made sure I would cook you dinner first."

"Of course." Good old unapologetic Vy.

Nadine had the best friends on earth. She stared at the check in her hand. Sam Carmichael was the fair owner's grandson. Now that he'd moved to town and had fallen in love with Vy, he had thrown himself into the rejuvenation wholeheartedly.

"With two thousand dollars, I can advertise even farther afield to get more people to attend."

"That's the idea."

"Thank Sam for me. Give him a big hug and kiss."

"Not a hardship. The man's a great kisser."

"TMI, Vy."

Nadine cleaned up the few plates in a matter of minutes and returned them to their spots in her tidy cupboards. She put on her running shoes and walked Vy out to Main Street. Vy got into her car to drive home. She and Sam lived on his grandfather's old homestead at the back of the fairgrounds.

In all the years Nadine had known Vy, she had never seen her so settled or so happy—and happiness looked good on her. It seemed to be spreading. The women on the revival committee were falling in love one after the other.

Way back in November, a stranger named Travis Read had come to town and had bought the old Victorian that Rachel McGuire had always wanted. How appropriate that they had fallen in love and were now married and living in the house with Rachel's two daughters.

In February, Travis's sister, Samantha, had landed on Michael Moreno's doorstep in a snowstorm with two boys in tow. Widower Michael's little girl and boy had become enamored with Samantha right away. It had taken a bit longer for Michael to fall for her, but when he did, he went down like a ton of bricks. They were now a blended family. Samantha, an accountant by trade, had taken over the committee's finances. She fit right in. Nadine was blessed to have added another friend to her slim posse.

Then Vy had fallen for Sam Carmichael, even though they'd had a rocky start. Former Wall Street business-man Sam had come to town pretending to be a cowboy, of all things. It hadn't taken Vy long to burst his phony bubble. Good thing it turned out that Sam liked feisty women. They lived with his tween daughter and were expecting their new baby just before Christmas.

In June, Honey Armstrong had fallen for Sheriff Cole Payette. No surprise there. He was a super good-looking, salt-of-the-earth guy who'd had a crush on Honey for years. So great that he'd finally acted on it. Of course, those two little children—he'd become their guardian after his sister and her husband died—had helped move things along faster. Nadine was so glad they'd all found love and joy amid such tragedy.

Of the six women on the committee, only Nadine and Max were single. Nadine knew she wasn't about to fall in love with anyone. She had her hands full trying to support herself...and now this trouble with Lee.

That left Maxine. Nadine frowned. What went on with Max? What had happened to her years ago that had left her bitter? What was broken there?

Max had never confided in any of them. She had a young son whose father was no longer around. He was the one bright spot in her life.

Nadine completed her walk around town, fifteen thousand steps by the time dusk fell and her old de-mons began to haunt her. Back in the quiet apartment, her worries closed in on her.

She curled up on the sofa with a word puzzle book, immersing herself in the logic of thinking a problem through and finding the right answer. Puzzles had clues. Clues led to answers and answers to solutions. Solutions brought order to chaos.

Tired, she fell into bed, but sleep eluded her. When it finally came sometime in the early morning, it brought troubled dreams. Again.

Her nightmares exhausted her.

She awoke with a startled exclamation, sweating, unable to remember what those dreams had been about. She could guess. Dear God, when would the sadness and fear end?

In the morning, she dressed in jeans and a denim shirt for her ride with Zach.

She stopped in at the office as she did every morning to log in to the news sites she followed and get the scoop on what was going on around the world. She hoped Lee wouldn't be in yet. He was.

She didn't know what to think of him, and how to feel when he had changed so much and yet still showed signs of the man she used to respect.

She'd decided she would pay his mother a visit. Nadine had always liked her. Maybe she could learn something without bothering Zach.

"I'll talk to your mother," Nadine said. "Is she at the Sunrise Home?"

Lee seemed to breathe a sigh, as though relieved. "Yes. So's Carson Carmichael. You could also see if he remembers anything."

Carson was the previous owner of the rodeo. Nadine had gotten to know him well through her work on the revival committee.

"He's not at the home anymore," she told Lee.

His eyebrows shot to his hairline. "Where is he?"

"His grandson, Sam, moved him to Carson's house on the fairgrounds. Sam and Violet live there, too."

"How did I miss that?"

Nadine grimaced. Lee liked to think he had his finger on the town's pulse, but that wasn't true. He rarely left the office or his home anymore. Nadine did all his legwork for him.

"It's recent," she said. "Vy and Sam brought him from Sunrise to his old house a couple of weeks ago. He's happy there now."

"What else are you doing today besides talking to my mom?"

"I'm interviewing Zach again."

"Then you'd better get out there to interview him right away."

"Sure."

"Go on now. I want that article in next week's issue. Or the one after at the latest."

The paper used to be issued daily, but Lee had gotten rid of a lot of their freelancers and had changed it to a weekly.

His one other reporter had retired and never been replaced. That left him and Nadine, with a part-timer Dave doing formatting and taking care of printing.

It all hinted at financial difficulty. No surprise. All newspapers faced insecurity these days.

Lee turned his attention to his email, as though dismissing her.

"One more thing." She told him about her idea for the paper to put on a writing contest for children. The idea had grown out of Aiden's desire to have his story published. What if they allowed all of the children in town the same opportunity to tell their stories?

"Why?" Lee asked.

"To promote the fair. It's only a month away. We could ask the children to write about their ranching experiences or Rodeo life, if they live in town."

Nadine's role on the revival committee was promotion. This would encourage more interest.

Lee mulled it over. "I like it. It would increase readership for the next month."

"We could say that we'll announce the winner on the last day of the fair. It would generate even more excitement."

"Okay. Let's do it." Lee sounded committed. "I'll write up an announcement for next week's paper and put up a poster in the window."

This was more like the Lee she used to know, accommodating and polite.

"Thank you," she said.

"I still want the Brandt story. Get it however you need to." His voice had slipped back into his new hard edge.

"Right," she said. In the middle of her sleepless night, she'd come up with a solution to her troublesome puzzle.

She had decided to put her heart into this story, because that was how she wrote every story. She couldn't avoid it. She was fighting for her job and for her future in Rodeo and in this newspaper office.

If she wrote it and somehow managed to give Lee what he wanted while she maintained her own integrity, she could keep her job, stay in town and someday take over the *Rodeo Wrangler*.

Stepping out of the office, she felt she could find a way to deal with Lee, her journalistic integrity and Zach's privacy.

She could do this. She could write a story that wouldn't hurt Zach.

She drove onto the Brandt ranch shortly before nine

with her nerves flaring and raw. While she might have come up with a fix, she didn't believe for a moment that it would be easy to pull off. Behind her dark sunglasses, the grit caused by last night's poor sleep hurt her eyes.

Zach and his two boys were already out in the yard waiting for her.

She stepped out of the car, but before she could reach back in to get her bag, both boys crowded her. They were physical little guys. One wrapped his arms around her waist, surprising her. The other patted her hip for her attention.

She looked helplessly at Zach.

"Boys, give Nadine room."

They stepped away from her, but both watched her with identical expressions of expectation. Why? Did they want her to guess who was who?

She studied them and, pointing first at one and then at the other, said, "Aiden. Ryan."

They giggled, yelled, "Yeah!" then ran away, racing around the car while Nadine looked to Zach for confirmation.

He started to say something, but one of the boys shouted, "No, Dad, don't tell her!"

He shook his head subtly so they wouldn't see. She'd gotten their names wrong. No wonder. They were dressed identically and had no obvious features to differentiate them.

And...they thought it was hilarious that she couldn't tell the difference. With Nadine's love of a good puzzle, she vowed to learn to tell them apart.

Zach spoke up. "They devised a little something for you."

Devised?

The boys stopped chasing each other around the car and stood in front of her.

"We made a mystery for you," one of them said.

Her spirits lifted. The boys were happy to see her and had *devised* something for her. "What do you mean? What kind of mystery?"

"You know," the other boy said. "The kind where you have to figure out the answer."

"I love puzzles, but you didn't know that. Why did you make a mystery?"

"Because you're a reporter. Dad said that means you try to figure out the truth."

"We like mysteries. Dad reads them to us at night."

Zach raised his shoulders. "I found some ancient Hardy Boys books in the attic. I know they're dated. No one reads them these days, but the boys like to guess the endings while I'm reading."

"I'm impressed," Nadine said, first because Zach was reading stories aloud to his sons—she *loved* that—but also because the twins had inquisitive minds.

Come to think of it, she hadn't seen either a TV or a computer in the house. She asked about that.

"Yeah, we got both."

"Have both, Ryan."

"I know. I just told the lady that."

Nadine shared a smile with Zach.

"They have both," Zach said, "but we don't do much screen time around here. I have nothing against technology. It's going to be important to their success in the future, but I like to find simple ways to encourage thought and open-mindedness."

Oh, good lord. A man like Zach could truly wiggle his way past every one of her hard-earned defenses and straight into her heart. She had known he was thoughtful, but now he was nurturing that trait in his active young sons.

Talk about attractive.

The thought of getting beneath his physically appealing exterior to the truth of the man made her own inquisitiveness perk up. She loved this part of the job as much as writing up the final story. But while she was fired up for the interview to begin, the cloud of Lee's demands threatened to block out the sun of her curiosity.

She could do this. She could write up a great article with no one getting hurt.

She remembered the mystery the boys had created for her and turned her attention to them.

"What are we waiting for? Let's get to that mystery."

Their matching smiles chased away all of those ugly clouds. They each took a sheet of paper out of the chest pocket of their little plaid shirts.

"You have to read mine first."

"After then you read mine."

She took both papers. "What are they?"

"Clues!" they said in unison.

She opened the first one to find two lines written in block letters.

WLAK TO THE OKE TREE ACROSS FROM THE HOUSE.
TURN TO THE ~~LEFT~~ RIGHT AND WALK FIFTY PACES.

"You have to do that first and then you can open Aiden's note." So obviously that was Ryan talking.

She walked to the oak with both boys on either side of her, Zach trailing behind. At the tree, she turned right and began to pace off the distance ordered in the note.

"Wait a minute," Zach said. "Stop."

She turned to him with a questioning eyebrow raised.

Zach put his hands on his sons' shoulders. "Who walked off these paces this morning?"

"I did."

"Okay, Ryan, you'd better walk them off now and we'll follow. Nadine's legs are a lot longer than yours so she'll end up overshooting wherever it is you want her to go."

The tips of his ears turned red as he averted his gaze from her legs. She might have read admiration there. She had no chance to ponder that possibility because Ryan caught her attention by starting to pace and count, his identical sidekick helping him before they broke into an argument when Ryan missed *eighteen* in his counting.

They ran back to the "oke" tree to start over.

"They were the best of friends," Zach said.

Nadine got the reference right away, smiled and finished for him. "They were the worst of friends."

Zach returned her smile.

The boys returned to the tree three more times to restart their counting before giving up, running to their intended destination and waving her over.

She hid her laughter. She glanced at Zach, at the hand over his mouth hiding his smile.

They stood on either side of a tree stump. "Don't look behind it until you read my clue." That was Aiden speaking, since she'd already read Ryan's paper. They made her sit on the stump before reading.

We like you. Will you stay with us?
Here's a little house.

No spelling mistakes in this clue from Aiden the author, but *stay* with them?

"Have you read this?" she asked Zach.

"No." She handed it to him. He read and then studied his boys. The smallest of smiles lit up his well-defined lips.

"I might know what it means, but why don't I let the boys tell you?"

They made her stand and look behind the stump.

"You have to move the grass around."

"I don't mind as long as there aren't too many bugs." That got the boys giggling.

"Of course there's bugs." She thought that was Ryan— Zach had corrected his grammar earlier.

A tiny yellow object peeked out between the grass blades. She picked up a small Monopoly game piece. A house.

Zach asked his sons, "What does this mean?"

"Can she come with us tomorrow night?" One of the boys threw himself against his father's legs.

"To the cabin?" the other pleaded.

Zach nodded as though he'd guessed the answer all along. "I don't know if she'd want to."

"Want to what?" Nadine asked.

"One night a week, the boys and I head out to our cabin and have a sleepover. They like it."

A sleepover? "Where's the cabin?" she asked.

"On Dad's mountain." Both boys pointed to the large hill Zach had been painting when she'd watched him in his studio yesterday.

"It's a one-room cabin the family built years ago in case ranch hands get stranded by weather." Zach stared off at the mountain and then returned his attention to his sons. "There are only two beds in there. Where would we all sleep?"

"We can use the air mattress!"

"We can put it on the floor."

"You've obviously thought this through," Zach said. Turning to Nadine, he asked, "What do you think? Are you game for camping out for one night in a rustic cabin?"

"Please!"

"Please."

One of the twins was quieter than the other. One spoke in exclamations. Maybe that was how she could learn to tell them apart. She wanted to. She didn't like thinking of them as just generic little boys without their own personalities.

But back to the issue at hand…stay with them in a cabin?

"Why?" she blurted.

"Because you have to get the next clue to the mystery there!"

And here she was, thinking she'd solved it already.

"Because we like you and it would be different."

"Yes, it sure would," Zach said. Nadine couldn't interpret his tone. Did he want her to say yes or no?

"Please!"

"Please?"

Two earnest little faces stared up at her. How could she say no?

"Okay."

"Yay!!!"

Aiden just beamed.

"Let's go get the horses ready for our ride," Zach said. He turned to her as the boys ran off toward the stable. "Sorry about that. They really put you on the spot. There's electricity, but no running water. Be prepared for that."

Nadine stared after them. "They barely know me.

Why would they want me to stay for a sleepover?" *And why would Zach?*

"I guess you left a good impression yesterday. Aiden said he liked that you didn't talk down to him. When you commented on his writing, he felt like a grown-up."

"That's only because I don't know how to talk to children."

"They seemed to think you got it just right."

Staying here overnight? Sleeping on the ranch? She didn't know... Maybe it would be okay. Would she be able to get Zach to open up about his family if the atmosphere was relaxed? She hoped she hadn't made a mistake in agreeing, but it could be exactly the opportunity she needed.

Zach led them back to the yard. "Get whatever you need for the interview. The lighter, the better. I'll saddle a couple of horses."

Nadine retrieved only the recorder that she'd recharged overnight.

Zach got the horses ready and brought them outside. Sunlight brought out the gold in his hazel eyes.

Dear Lord, the man had great eyes.

He boosted Nadine onto her horse, mounted his own and they ambled out of the yard. Well, the adults ambled. The twins set off at a brisk trot on their ponies.

"They'll ride ahead for a while if you want to start interviewing me," Zach offered.

That was a relief. She hadn't considered that the boys would be around all day. Nadine turned on her recorder and held it out toward Zach. "I'm curious about where your love of painting came from. Does Rick paint? Did your grandfather?"

"No to both questions."

"So how did it spring up in you, from a vacuum?"

"I can't answer that question. You're asking the wrong person."

She frowned. "Who should I be asking?"

A funny smile hovered on Zach's lips. "I guess that would depend on your belief system. The answer could be God or Buddha or Yahweh, or…you get my drift. I guess my talent came to me from a higher power. I can't say it was instilled in me by my parents. It was just already there. I was born with the talent and the desire to paint."

"Aiden seems to have inherited some of your creativity."

"True."

"Did Ryan?"

"Not in an artistic way, at least. Ryan isn't a child who wants to sit still for long. He's physical. I think his talents will be in sports or athletics. But he's only seven, so a lot can change."

Zach pulled up short. Nadine stopped her own horse. "Look at the light on the mountain," he said. "This is the most beautiful spot on earth. There is no place lovelier."

Here was a chance to find out more about Zach. Why was this land so important to him? "How can you possibly know that when you've only ever lived *here*? You would have to travel and see the world to know that definitively."

His steady gaze unnerved her.

"Otherwise, it's a personal preference," she continued, playing devil's advocate. "You can't possibly know when you've never been outside of Rodeo, Montana."

"How do you know?"

"It just makes sense. If you haven't seen the world outside of your own backyard—"

"I meant, how do you know I haven't been outside of Rodeo?"

That got Nadine thinking. "You mean you've traveled?"

"Extensively."

"Really? Where?" She kept the tape rolling even though this didn't relate to painting directly. In fact, when interviewing a subject, she never turned it off. You never knew where a conversation could lead and what you might learn.

He stared out across his land. "I took two years away from the ranch, packed a backpack and hitchhiked through Tibet and the Himalayas." His gaze focused and returned to her. "It was all stunning. Every place I visited was beautiful. I liked being exposed to cultures that were profoundly different from my own. I liked all of the unusual foods. Unusual to me, at any rate."

"Did you paint?"

"I photographed. After I came home, I used those photos to paint some of the most spectacular scenery on this earth."

"But I haven't seen any of those paintings around town."

"No, and you won't. Those are mine. They belong to me and to my sons someday."

She envied him that experience. She'd only gone as far as New York. Every morning she went online to keep in touch with the world. He had actually gone out into it.

"So you saw Tibet and the Himalayas. Is that all you have to compare to Rodeo?"

"I trekked into China. Amazing countryside there. I came back west across India and Pakistan. I found that I experienced the countries with more than just my painter's eye. Every sense came alive. Every country smelled dif-

ferent. I made my way across Turkey and Greece. I back-
packed across Europe and ended up in Spain."

The pause in his narrative seemed significant, but she
didn't know why. She raised an eyebrow.

"I met my wife in Spain."

Oh. His wife.

Chapter Four

It was obvious to Zach that Nadine hadn't known his wife was Spanish. She hadn't known about his travels, either. It was also obvious, painfully so, that he hadn't been more than a footnote in her life while she was away.

Not that he had expected much, and he'd never assumed that he meant much to her. But the town wasn't that large. Had she washed her hands of Rodeo so thoroughly when she left that she hadn't asked about anyone or even heard the slightest gossip?

Everyone he'd talked to, all of her friends, had thought she'd shaken off the dust of sleepy little old Rodeo, Montana, for the neon jungle of New York City for good. Even so, had the people of Rodeo meant nothing? Had the town been so insignificant? If that was the case, why had she come back?

He'd heard that she reported stories live for a television station in New York City. That was impressive. So why was she back here working for Lee and writing human interest stories for a small regional newspaper? After the Big Apple, wasn't it a huge letdown?

"Do you want to talk about her?" Nadine asked.

Good question. Did he?

Maria had left him three years ago, with their uncontested divorce following immediately. She had signed over full custody of the boys to Zach without a word of objection. It felt like only yesterday. It also felt like ancient history.

The breakdown of his marriage still left him feeling like a failure. Could he have done more?

"Her name is Maria," he said. "I fell for her right away." *Fell for her.* Massive understatement. "If you want to know what she looks like, she's right there." He pointed to his two sons riding ahead on their ponies.

"What was she like?"

"Intelligent. Passionate. Clever. She had—has—a wicked sense of humor." For a moment, he lost himself in the memory of her smile.

"Did you live there or come home immediately?"

"We came to Rodeo a couple of days after the wedding."

"So you married in Spain?"

"Yes. She was excited about coming here. She never made a word of protest about leaving her home country, but—" He remembered the recorder. "You're still recording, aren't you?"

She nodded. "Would you rather I didn't?"

"Turn it off now. This isn't about just me. It's also about the boys."

She turned it off.

"But—?" Nadine prompted.

"But she was never happy here. She'd thought she would see more of the big cities. I never lied to her, though. I described Rodeo to her before we came. I was honest about where we would live."

"That wasn't enough for her?"

"No. She started to ask when we were going to visit San Francisco and New York." He glanced at her. "She had a lot of curiosity about big city life."

"And yet you had never deceived her. You had told her she was coming here to live a rural life."

"Correct. In ways, she had deceived me. Apparently, she had told her mother she knew she could talk her way around me. That she could not only visit, but live the life she wanted in America. Not the one I wanted to give her."

"That was dishonest of her."

"Yes. I had fallen for her hard, but I was still me."

"Meaning that you were stubborn."

He shot her a hard glare, but she was smiling and he softened. "I like to think of it as determined."

"So did you ever take her anywhere?"

"To San Francisco once. She loved it and wanted to stay there. We argued. I asked why she had married me if she didn't want to live in my home. She said a home is anywhere you make it."

Nadine tucked her recorder into her pocket. "I guess there's a certain amount of truth in that."

"There is, but I had already traveled for two years. I had seen amazing places and things. I had learned that I loved Rodeo and this ranch more than anywhere else on earth. This land was a deeply ingrained part of me. I made no bones about that when I met her. In fact, I was on my way home when we met."

"It must have been a whirlwind romance." Nadine seemed to be genuinely interested.

"I extended my holiday by four months. I got to know her. I got to know her family. I wanted to understand who she was. She assured me she would welcome the ranching life."

"But she really just wanted to see America? She wanted a more exciting life than the one she had?"

Zach struggled to restrain the old anger and speak

objectively. "In a nutshell, yes, which makes her sound dishonest, but I think she did love me. I believe that still. She just thought she could change me."

Nadine frowned. "Believing you can change a person is not a great way to start a marriage. Or so I would think. I have no experience in that area."

He shrugged. "Experience or not, you hit the nail on the head." He called out to his boys that it was time to go back. "Sorry," he said. "I have ranch chores to do this afternoon." He heard his boys turn their horses and begin trotting behind him.

He hadn't known about their plans to invite Nadine to the cabin tomorrow night. It was perfect, though. Couldn't be better.

He wanted Nadine in his life. He needed to get her out to his ranch as often as possible to see how she felt about the ranch, to get to know her, so she could get to know him, and so he could nurture a second chance that felt right. And though he hadn't told the twins anything about that, they were already helping his cause.

"So…what happened?" Nadine prompted him. "She just left one day?"

He didn't really want to keep talking about Maria, that chapter of his life in many ways still raw. But shouldn't he give Nadine a glimpse into his past—and his children's history—if he hoped to have a relationship with her?

She'd come out to his ranch yesterday and his old feelings for her had flooded him. He wanted to get to know her better. That meant he had to share parts of himself he usually held close.

"She left, yeah. This might sound strange," he said, "but I kept in touch with her father. I liked the man a lot. We talked about farming and ranching. We were kindred spirits. He later confessed that he'd had doubts about his daughter marrying me."

"He didn't think you deserved her?"

At the astonishment in her voice, gratification coursed through Zach. She might not have romantic feelings for him, but she admired him.

They could work on the romance later.

"It was the other way around," Zach said. "He loved his daughter, but she had spent so many years complaining that she was meant for bigger and better things than rural Spain, he was surprised when she said she wanted to marry me and come home to my ranch. Maria's mother, on the other hand, had understood and agreed with her plans and thought they would work. She believed I would set up a house for Maria in a big city. I don't know what they thought I would do for work when my training and talent is here on the land. How would I support us in a city? How did they think I would be able to afford a house in a city like New York?"

"They saw you as a landowner, Zach. That would signify a certain amount of wealth. Ownership of this much land could lead others to believe you are well off."

Zach bit back his exasperation. "The land isn't mine. Not yet, anyway. It belongs to my father. How could I sell my father's land? I told Maria that every time she argued that we should move."

"What was her response?"

"That we should get Rick to sell and give us the proceeds. She kept mentioning his age. My dad has a lot of good years left in him. It was far too early to be farming him out, so to speak."

"Did you resent her for that?"

"Absolutely. My dad was not, never has been and never will be disposable." Love for his father swamped him.

"I'm guessing things didn't get better when the twins were born."

After that observation, Zach realized what he should have guessed all along...that Nadine was a good interviewer, even if she wasn't technically interviewing him at the moment. She asked all of the right questions to get to the heart of the story.

If only his life, and the tragedy of his divorce, had been just a story instead of reality. Ryan and Aiden took turns chasing each other across a field, their laughter bright enough to rival the sunshine bathing his land, reminding Zach of the good that had come out of his history.

"Things did not get better, no. I was ecstatic she gave birth, but the babies made Maria feel trapped. I tried hard, real hard, to support her, but once she came to the understanding that our life was never going to change—at least not in the way she wanted it to—she decided to go back home to Spain."

The boys passed them on their ponies. Zach waited until they were out of hearing range before continuing.

Staring at the boys, Nadine said, "Zach, that's so sad. I'm sorry."

He couldn't respond to her sadness. He'd lived through too much of it himself. "I wondered how she could leave her children. She said she missed her family. Her own family. But the boys are *ours*, not just mine. It made me sad, but also angry."

"And the boys?" Nadine asked. "Are they with you full-time?"

He didn't usually talk about himself so much, but it seemed that once the floodgates had opened he couldn't stop. "She gave me full custody and I didn't fight her on it, as much as my heart broke for the boys. They'll always have to grapple with the fact of their mom leaving them. I'd do anything to protect them from that pain. But I like to think I'm doing an okay job of raising them."

He kicked his horse into a faster trot. He didn't want Nadine to think he needed assurances on that point. "She just wanted to go home."

Nadine caught up to him. "How long ago was that?"

"Three years."

"Do you ever hear from her?"

"Occasionally she emails or sends texts. Every couple of months, she Skypes with the boys."

"Did she remarry?"

"Yes. He has money. They have a beautiful home in Madrid. It's the marriage she should have made the first time around."

"Except that she fell in love with an American rancher."

"It might have been better for her if I had never passed through Spain on my way home."

"For her, maybe, but not for you. You have two amazing sons." She smiled, and he felt a flicker of pride—and hope. She liked his boys.

And she seemed to understand. Yes, marrying Maria had been a mistake for him as a man, but a miracle for him as a father.

They rode into the yard.

"You're going to get to know the boys a lot better tomorrow night." He helped her to dismount. For a moment, she looked blank. She'd forgotten. "The sleepover?"

Her smile slipped. "Oh, yes. The sleepover."

"Do you want to cancel?" he asked, following her gaze to the boys as they brushed their ponies, their exuberance not the least bit dimmed by the long ride.

She shook her head and Zach was relieved she wouldn't disappoint them. They'd already had more than their share of disappointment in their young lives.

"I guess we didn't talk much about my paintings today." He took off his cowboy hat and swiped a cotton handkerchief across the back of his neck. The day had turned hot.

"That's okay. I need to understand who you are as a man to write about your paintings."

"Does it usually take this long to get to know your subjects?"

"Yes. I give it as much time and attention as I need to, and as many meetings as it takes. I don't speculate. I don't make up anything."

Good. She would be coming out to the ranch a number of times, giving him plenty of opportunity to advance his goal to…what? Woo her? Court her? What was the current term? "Go after her" sounded crass and stalker-ish.

He'd wanted to ask her out since she'd returned to town, but the sticking point had been the ranch, and the way she'd disliked it as a teen.

He needed to see if her attitude toward ranching, his ranch in particular, had changed. He'd taken one woman away from her true goals. He couldn't do it to another.

She'd seemed to enjoy the ride today.

Or maybe she'd just liked getting to know him better. For himself, or for the article?

He watched her walk away and swiped the handkerchief across his forehead.

He'd turned himself inside out in reliving his marriage and divorce. Maybe he'd told Nadine too much.

NADINE DIDN'T BOTHER going back to the newspaper office. She didn't want to run into Lee.

She did a fair amount of the actual writing in her apartment anyway. Lee wouldn't miss her.

She'd thought about his threat to fire her. She was his only reporter. Knowing Lee, he would go ahead and hire someone fresh out of a small college somewhere in one of the western states, someone who would be happy to gain experience anywhere.

She didn't fool herself into thinking she couldn't be replaced.

Her thoughts turned to Zach and all that he'd shared with her. Off the record, yes, and she would keep it that way.

She hadn't known a thing about what had gone on with Zach while she was gone. She hadn't heard much about any of the town's news. Why hadn't her friends shared more with her when she'd been away?

Almost as soon as the thought popped into her head, she knew her answer.

They had thought she hadn't cared. In large measure, they'd been right. It wasn't as if she'd asked. As much as she'd liked Rodeo and the people living here, and as much as she had adored her friends, all of the good had been tainted by living with her aunt. At the time, she hadn't realized what a truly mean-spirited woman she was.

Nadine had come out of the experience wanting to run away from Rodeo as far and as fast as she could. Now, at twenty-nine and with her aunt dead, she saw the town in a different light.

Zach's story had fascinated her—renewed her distaste in what she had to do—and made her more determined than ever to learn what this big secret was and then to deal with it with discretion.

Was she fooling herself? Revealing someone's secret had nothing to do with discretion.

Zach might seem solid and self-confident, but she'd sensed deep hurt while he talked about his ex-wife. The man had been wildly in love with his bride, no doubt full of pride in her and in the land he'd brought her home to.

Nadine could imagine the scene.

Look. This is where I grew up. Someday, this will be ours, as far as the eye can see. Someday, it will belong to our children. Isn't it beautiful?

But Maria had chosen to leave, rejecting him, his land and most importantly their children. How that must have devastated a man like Zach, who would never turn his back on his responsibilities. Nadine had never met the woman, but knew she did not deserve Zach. He deserved only the best. She hoped someday he would find the love he merited.

She drove straight to the nursing home to visit Lee's mother, to get this nastiness over with as quickly as possible and to deal with it as best she could.

At the reception desk, she asked whether she could see Norma Beeton. A nurse walked her to the far corner of the massive first floor and into a small private bedroom, cozy and prettily decorated.

Norma sat in a wheelchair beside a window, sunlight streaming through her silver cloud of hair and alighting on a soft pink scalp.

Lee had mentioned her age. Ninety-two. She looked every one of those years. A tiny woman, her spine curved forward, her right hand curled unnaturally, while her left looked only marginally better. Her purple-veined feet, clad in fluffy pink slippers, sat on padded footrests.

Having no idea what the state of Norma's mind might be at the moment, Nadine introduced herself.

Norma smiled politely after the introduction, but didn't seem to recognize her.

Lee's father had started the paper decades ago and Norma had been involved as well, mainly in a secretarial role, but she'd also had an abiding interest in journalism. By the time Nadine had arrived on the scene as a teen working in the afternoons after school Norma had already retired. She did, however, visit regularly while Nadine worked there. They'd gotten to know each other. She had encouraged Nadine in her pursuit of journalism as a career and had even applauded when she'd been accepted into college out east.

But here, now, it was obvious that Norma didn't remember her. How sad.

As Norma listened with a polite, puzzled frown, Nadine explained who she was, leaving out that she worked for Lee given their falling out, saying only that she was researching the Brandt family. She asked her about Judith Brandt, Zach's grandmother.

"What did you say your name was again?"

"Nadine Campbell."

"I used to know a girl named Nadine. She had curly hair."

"That was me. I straighten my hair now."

Norma looked like she was trying to place Nadine in her mind. "That was you? The girl I knew?"

"Yes."

Norma seemed to accept that, so Nadine asked, "Can you tell me about Judith Brandt?"

She said, "I knew a girl named Judith. She was my best friend. Her name was Collins. Not Brandt. She was going to marry Harvey Broome."

She was? Judith was going to marry a Broome? That was news to Nadine. But Judith didn't marry a Broome. She married Zach's grandfather.

"Was she engaged to Harvey?"

"Who?"

Oh, dear. It was going to be that kind of conversation.

"Was Judith engaged to Harvey Broome?"

"Why, yes, she was."

"Then why did she marry Richard?"

"She fell in love with him," Norma said as though the answer was obvious.

"Harvey must not have been happy about it."

"Lord, no. There was that incident, you know."

"What incident?"

"The fight between Richard and Harvey just after Richard stole Judith away and married her. Harvey was furious."

Nadine became alert. Was this the secret? The men had fought? But why was that so bad?

"Harvey died, of course," Norma said.

Say what? *Died?*

"Was it because of the fight?"

"Yes, of course."

There was no *of course* about it. Was she coming close to finding out the secret? But what exactly *was* the secret? How Harvey had died?

As a journalist, she'd learned to be skeptical. Norma wasn't giving her much to go on and there was no guarantee her memories were sound or accurate.

"Can you tell me about the fight?" Nadine asked.

"Harvey and Richard both loved Judith. She was a beautiful girl." A trace of bitterness crept into Norma's voice and Nadine wondered how good a friend she had really been to Zach's grandmother.

"At first she was with Harvey, but then changed her mind and wanted Richard. She married him. I don't know why she stopped loving Harvey, but she sure ended up being crazy about Richard. She loved him until the day she died twenty years later."

That timeline seemed right for Judith's death. Nadine would have to confirm Norma's story, but at least she knew the older woman was keeping some facts straight.

"What happened between Harvey and Richard?"

"Judith made her decision to stop seeing Harvey and marry Richard quickly. It left Harvey confused, hurt and angry. Oh, dear goodness, was he angry. He told me he wanted to kill Richard for stealing his girl. There was a lot of bad blood between the two families after that."

Norma stared out of the window, eyes unfocused as though caught up in the past. Nadine waited her out.

"One night," she said a few minutes later, "Harvey said he wanted to meet Richard out at the old quarry. Richard knew he wanted to fight. Judith told him not to go, but you know men and their pride. If this had been another time and place, they would have probably had a duel and one of them would have killed the other."

But one of them *had* died that night. Norma had just said so.

"What happened?" Nadine asked, careful to keep her tone neutral.

"Richard went and there was some terrible yelling, I tell you."

"How do you know?"

"I was there."

Nadine just about dropped her recorder. "What?"

"I went for Judith's sake. She was worried Harvey might hurt Richard badly. She shouldn't have worried. Richard held his own, all right."

"Was he violent?" Nadine couldn't imagine one of Zach's ancestors being violent. On the other hand, she'd hate to see someone try to hurt Zach's boys. He would protect them at any cost.

"Only as much as Harvey was," Norma said. "There weren't any weapons. Just their fists. But they were both getting tired. Harvey took a swing at Richard and Richard stepped out of the way. Harvey lost his footing and fell. He stayed down. Richard was saying, 'Harvey, get up and fight,' but Harvey didn't move. Richard shook his shoulder. Harvey still didn't move."

Norma took a drink from a plastic cup with a straw, wrinkles fanning like the sun's rays around her pursed lips. Nadine considered how real it was all sounding. It could be true.

"That's when I came out from my hiding spot. Richard was glad to see me. We both realized that Harvey had tripped on a rock and had gone down hard, hitting his head on another rock. We figured, and so did the coroner later, that he died instantly. There was nothing either of us could do."

Dear God. Nadine would have to verify this. Somewhere in the newspaper's archives there had to be articles about it. If it was true, how tragic.

"Richard and I left him there and drove to the old gas station that used to be out on 29 and called the sheriff's office. There was a full investigation and Richard was cleared of wrongdoing. Still, it would have been hard to prove it if I hadn't seen the whole thing."

Thank God Norma had been there or Zach's grandfather might have gone to prison for murder and that would have made the situation even more tragic.

"How many people knew about the fight?" she asked.

"The whole town knew," Norma said, thus dashing Nadine's hope that this was the secret.

If not the fight, and Harvey's death, then what? Had Richard done anything else to the Broomes that could have been part of the big, bad secret?

"Is that all you know about what went on between Richard and the Broomes?"

Norma looked confused. "I think so. After Harvey's death, the families hated each other, but there were no more fistfights or any other violence that I ever heard of."

How exactly was Nadine supposed to get the secret out of Norma? Maybe all she had to do was ask.

"Norma, Lee seems to think there's a big, dark secret about Richard. Would you know anything about that?"

"Lee," Norma scoffed. "Maybe if I'd married Richard myself instead of Lee's father, Lee might have been a better man. That Rick is nice. I always liked him."

She'd liked Zach's father, Rick, better than her own son? Maybe part of Lee's problem was sitting right here in front of Nadine. Lee wasn't a stupid man. He had to know that he had disappointed his own mother somehow. Had it led to Lee's unhappiness?

Norma's gaze turned inward again. "Lee's father did have that nice newspaper office, though. I always wanted to be a reporter." She swung back to Nadine. "Women these days have more opportunities than we had."

It seemed that the walk down memory lane had ended. Despite changing the questions and her repeated attempts to get answers out of Norma, the woman seemed to have spent enough time in the past.

Nadine left a short while later.

Walking through the hallway and passing rooms filled with Rodeo's oldest citizens, an idea for a series of articles developed.

Wouldn't it be great to tell Rodeo's history through the eyes of the people who had lived it?

This was the kind of thing that fired her up about journalism…telling people's stories.

When she drove back to town and entered the newspaper office, she found it blessedly empty. She really didn't want to see Lee again today.

She sat at her computer and wrote bits and pieces for her article, mainly impressions of who she thought Zach was. She started her research into his family's background. She needed to read the full story of what had happened between those two men. She spooled through microfiche of old articles and found plenty about the fight, Harvey's death and the inquest. Richard was indeed cleared of any wrongdoing.

Harvey had initiated the fight. Neither Richard nor Norma had moved the body, so Harvey's head still sat on the rock that had killed him by the time the authorities had arrived. A freak accident, it was called.

Nadine continued to scroll until she hit upon an article that featured photographs of the two men.

And gasped.

She stared at the photograph of Harvey Broome. It couldn't be possible. It *couldn't*. Why didn't everyone in town know this?

How on earth could she ask Zach about it?

Harvey had died so young, and Rick must look so much like his mother that perhaps no one in Zach's generation knew…

But did Zach? And how could Nadine find out without actually asking him, "Which one of those men was your real grandfather?"

Chapter Five

That night, Nadine awoke sweaty and disoriented, with a headache pounding behind her right eye. She thought she might have been moaning. No wonder she was reluctant to stay overnight with two young boys and a grown man. A very attractive man.

Her nightmares were too frequent.

What if she had one tonight and woke up the boys?

But she'd already promised them.

Since coming back to Rodeo, she'd had no boyfriends, not even a one-night stand because she didn't want anyone staying over. If Vy knew, she would tell Nadine it was unnatural to go so long without sex.

Oh, who was Nadine kidding? Vy probably already knew that Nadine spent every night alone.

There was no one in Rodeo with whom she would let down her guard. There was certainly no one with whom she would consider having a relationship. So she lived alone.

Some would say she lived a barren life. Some would be right. Her aunt, if she were alive, would tell her it was what she deserved.

Nadine glanced at the clock. Four thirty.

No way would she get any more sleep tonight. She got up and curled in an armchair in the living room with her latest book of puzzles. Two hours later, she showered, comforted by the knowledge that the boys probably went to sleep early, so she would as well when she was at the cabin tonight.

She drove out to the ranch with mixed feelings. She liked the boys a lot already and knew she could have fun with them. Still, her mind worried the puzzle of the Brandt family secret like a wound that should be left to heal on its own.

Was she right in her suspicion? Was it better to bring it out into the open? Was it better to leave it hidden underground?

But then there was Lee and his threat.

Her stomach roiled.

She parked and approached Zach and his boys, her burgeoning suspicion of what the family secret might be burrowing under her skin. Zach's face was pretty much all of the proof she needed.

How was it that Lee had never guessed? Harvey had died long before Lee was born, so maybe it was plausible...

Rick came out of the house with a cooler bag that Nadine assumed held food for the night. One look at his face confirmed that he looked nothing like Harvey Broome. Did he just get all of his mother's looks and nothing from his father?

The headache threatened a return performance. She was tired. She would like nothing better than to forget about the article, Lee Beeton's needs and Zach's deep, dark family secrets.

The twins ran over and wrapped their arms around her.

"You came!"

"We're gonna make s'mores at the cabin."

"We got fishing poles!"

"I wrote another story."

This was exactly what Nadine needed. Blessedly uncomplicated bliss. What a couple of cuties. In only two days, they'd worked their way past her discomfort. She could be herself with them and that was good enough.

They liked her just the way she was.

The boys lifted her spirits and she made a spur-of-the-moment decision.

For today and this evening, she would just enjoy. Tonight would be a break from reporting and interviewing and speculation about a thing that could tear apart Zach's world if he didn't already know. She was going to give herself over to enjoying the boys.

Aiden and Ryan said goodbye to their grandfather.

"Will you be okay by yourself?" one twin asked quietly, so Nadine thought it might be Aiden.

"Yup, I'll be fine. Just like I am every time you go to the cabin." Rick smiled and waved them on their way.

They piled into Zach's pickup truck and drove to the cabin, which sat partway up his mountain.

"I know the names of all the trees!" There was definitely an exclamation mark at the end of that sentence.

"Ryan," she said.

"Yeah?" he answered.

She was right!

Zach caught her eye and smiled.

"Do you want me to tell you them?" Ryan asked. He was wearing a white T-shirt, like his dad. Aiden was wearing a dark blue shirt. Unless the boys switched their shirts, Nadine was good for the afternoon. All bets were off tomorrow morning when they put on different clothes.

"Later, Ryan," Zach said. "We'll have plenty of time

to explore and show Nadine around. First, we unpack the truck."

Nadine grabbed groceries and her overnight bag. Zach carried in bottles of water. The boys took bags of chips and marshmallows. In her opinion, they had enough food to last an entire week, not just one night, but then she tended to be frugal these days.

The cabin was a surprise. Rugged, yes, and small, but well stocked even without the food Rick had packed. At one end of the room was a large hearth, bracketed by plenty of dry wood on one side and a beat-up old armoire on the other. Not that they would need heat. It was nearing the end of July so the nights were still warm.

Tucked into a corner of the cabin was what could be described as a kitchen only with a great deal of charity. On a small counter stood a hot plate and an electric kettle. Pots and pans hung from hooks on the wall. Two particleboard cupboards cozied up against a full-size fridge. In front of that was a round table with four old ladder-back chairs.

Against each wall was a single bed.

"You sleep on that bed!" Ryan pointed to the far bed.

"Dad will sleep on the other one and me and Ryan will have the air mattress."

The air mattress would fill the space between the two beds. There was no other spot for it. Once it was blown up and in place, it was going to be a cozy room for sleeping.

She got nervous worrying about the coming night and her dreams before pulling herself together.

Have fun. Just for once, let go and have fun.

With the boys pulling her this way and that to show her the contents of the armoire that the ranch hands used and all the snacks they'd brought for later, it was easy enough for Nadine to distract herself from her fears.

She eyed the counters, piled with chips, popcorn, pop, marshmallows, chocolate and graham wafers for s'mores.

"Cabin nights are our let-loose nights," Zach explained. "The boys are allowed as many treats as they like because they're so good the other six days of the week."

"And we get to have a campfire going," Aiden said. Zach nodded. "Even in the middle of summer, it can get cool enough out here at night to allow for a fire. Though it's mainly to cook the s'mores."

"Let's go for a walk, Dad."

"Let's fish!"

"We'll do both," Zach said.

They left the cabin. The boys ran ahead.

"Have you ever gone fishing?" Zach asked.

"No. I grew up in a city. When I moved here, my aunt kept me pretty busy."

She'd been born and raised in Tucson before coming to Rodeo.

Zach nodded and would have asked more, Nadine was certain of it, but the boys drew his attention.

"I can show you how to put a worm on the hook," Aiden said.

"Sorry to get all squeamish on you, but I really don't like to handle worms. Or insects. Or snakes," she added for good measure.

"I'll do it for you!"

"Thanks, Ryan, I appreciate it."

They followed the boys to a stream.

"How can you have electricity this far from the ranch house?" Nadine asked, wondering about the logistics of having a cabin in an isolated location. This kind of thing was foreign to her and she found herself vastly curious.

Zach pointed past the stream. "There's a road a mile that way. It supplies electricity to the Broomes on the other side of the mountain. About twenty years ago, Dad paid to have a line run to the cabin to provide more comfort for the ranch hands."

The afternoon that followed was about as happy a time as Nadine had ever spent, amazing and unusual for her to kick back outdoors, to lie under a tree with a fishing pole in her hand, listening to Zach interact with his boys. Their pipsqueak voices contrasted with his deep rumble.

A large, warm hand touched her shoulder. *Zach.* Slowly she opened her eyes. Above her, yellow-green leaves shimmered like lace in front of a deep blue sky.

"What—?"

Beside her, Zach said, "You fell asleep." Already, after visiting him only—what?—two, three times, she knew his touch? How was that possible?

The twins ran up to them. "We're hungry!"

"We're going back to the cabin."

Nadine rubbed her eyes. "I'm sorry I nodded off."

"Nothing to worry about," Zach said. "You're here to relax."

They walked back to the cabin, Nadine trailing behind Zach, who carried all four fishing rods on his broad shoulders.

"Did we catch anything?" Nadine asked.

"Naw. Boys, run ahead and open the door to air out the cabin." When they were a distance ahead, Zach said, "There's nothing to catch in that stream."

Nadine stopped walking. "Then why on earth do you make the boys fish there?"

"First off, I don't *make* them. The first time we fished there, it was their idea. Second, it relaxes them. They're active boys and get wound up. It's good to find something calming for them to do." He reached back a hand to help her over a stump. Oh, yes, she was getting used to his touch. "When we come up here in the fall, Aiden gathers leaves to take home to show his Pop while Ryan looks for sleepy bees to study."

What a great life those boys had with Zach. It brought back childhood memories of her relationship with her mother, but those made her sad.

Today, she was bound and determined to be happy. Sadness was not allowed.

Back inside the cabin, the boys were already pulling hot dogs out of the fridge. In the fire pit outside, Ryan had firewood stacked and waited to put a match to it.

"Did you build that yourself?" Nadine studied his handiwork.

"Both my boys know how to build a fire."

"We're learning a lot of skills from Dad." Aiden stood beside his brother.

"Next summer, Dad's going to take us wilderness camping and teach us survival skills."

Sometimes these young boys sounded like miniature adults.

"That's amazing, Ryan." Nadine was truly impressed.

"Ready, Dad?" Ryan asked.

Zach nodded and handed him a box of long matches. Ryan took one out and made sure the top was closed before striking the match on the bottom. He put the flame to the kindling in several spots before tossing in the match.

"Well done, son," Zach said. "Go find us some sticks, boys."

They ran around scrounging for sticks that were just the right length.

Nadine followed Zach's lead in getting condiments out of the fridge and setting out old plates and cutlery on the table, all of which had seen better days.

They sat around the fire pit on upright logs.

Lunch was hot dogs roasted on sticks on the fire. It was delicious. Hot dogs! Eating outdoors seemed to make everything taste better.

Zach knocked down the fire.

In the afternoon, they hiked halfway up the side of the mountain. From afar, it looked like a gentle hill. Up close and personal, it was very much a mountain. Nadine stopped and turned around to look out over the countryside and...totally, suddenly, completely *got* Zach and his love of his land.

Montana stretched wide and beautiful as far as she could see. Golden fields basked in the July sunshine. A cloudless blue sky smiled down on a stunning landscape.

She felt Zach's eyes on her. She turned to him.

They said nothing. What was there to say? Words were inadequate. But they smiled in perfect communion.

Nadine didn't know if she had ever felt so close to another person as she did to Zach in that moment.

"Tomorrow, if you can come out again, we'll ride around to the other side of the mountain. There's something you should see. Okay?"

"Sure." Her voice came out shaking. Why was she so emotional today?

It would mean another day away from the office, but she would compensate by interviewing Zach again while they rode.

The boys ran up with things to give her. A stone

shaped like a heart and an old leaf that had turned to lace. Little boy treasures for a woman they liked.

She choked up. Such a simple thing, but she was unaccustomed to receiving gestures of affection. She had spent too many years on the receiving end of insults. She pushed her sunglasses up high onto her nose and started back downhill.

Back at the cabin, they began to prepare dinner. Apparently little boys didn't like to wait long between meals. On the other hand, Nadine realized when she checked her watch that they'd been walking for three hours.

Dinner was hamburgers made from ground beef and little else. Zach fried them in a pan.

"The boys don't like a lot of spices or 'weird things' in their burgers," Zach said. "Their description. I can try to tart them up somehow." He checked cupboards for spices, but Nadine stopped him.

"Plain is good. For me, burgers are all about the condiments. Do you have dill pickles?"

Zach reached into the fridge and pulled out a full bottle.

Nadine smiled. "Perfect."

Evening was settling in and Aiden built up kindling in the fireplace. Zach supervised while he lit the match and they toasted the buns for dinner. There were no vegetables or salad with the burgers.

"Nope. They get cabin night off from vegetables," Zach told her when she inquired.

All in all, it was one of the best meals she'd ever had. She laughed and Zach shot her a puzzled look.

"It isn't gourmet food, but it sure is good."

"Yeah!" Ryan agreed.

Again, thoughts of her mother intruded. What would

Nadine's life have been like if her mother hadn't died when she was only eleven? Better. So much better. The sadness that had plagued her for the past year threatened to overwhelm her.

Aiden came and stood in front of her. He put a hand on her knee. "Okay?" he asked. Such a sensitive little guy.

Oh, these sweet, amazing boys. Zach was a first-class, kick-ass father. She'd never met a better one.

She'd never known her real father, but her stepfather had been a loving man until both he and her mother had died.

Aiden watched her with worry in his dark chocolate eyes in an angelic face. Nadine's smile turned genuine. "I couldn't be more okay at this moment if I tried." She clapped her hands. "Is it time for s'mores?"

The boys ran to get the ingredients.

Again, Nadine was determined to make this a happy night for herself. To *be* happy. Of the four people in the cabin, only she knew what a Herculean task that was. She gave herself over to it and ate far too many s'mores before giving up on toasting and eating big fluffy marshmallows straight from the bag.

She didn't allow herself treats. Never candy.

It felt *awesome* to not hold back. She'd been ruthless in her self-discipline for too long.

She grinned and Zach grinned right back.

They played cards for most of the evening before blowing up the air mattress. There was barely room to move around it.

The boys got dressed and ready for bed first. Nadine squeezed into the miniscule washroom next. It held only a composting toilet, a huge bottle of hand sanitizer, and a bucket of clean water and another bucket for used water On the walls, the only decoration was an old mirror with the silver scratched off the back in places. She changed into a pair of sweats and a T-shirt, with her bra still on. Once she got into bed and they turned off the lights, she'd take it off for sleeping.

Tonight she was doing something she *never* did. She was going to leave on her makeup. She'd worn waterproof mascara that wouldn't smudge while she slept.

No way was she letting Zach see her without makeup.

She dumped her used water from brushing her teeth outside the front door.

Zach went last. When he came out of the bathroom, both boys were asleep on his bed instead of on the air mattress on the floor.

He picked up one of them. Now that the boys were in matching pajamas and sound asleep, Nadine no longer knew which was which.

Zach turned to place him on the mattress.

A man holding his sleeping child. Was there a more beautiful sight on this earth? She felt like crying again. What was *wrong* with her?

After settling both boys and tucking them in, Zach turned off the lights and banked the fire.

"Goodnight," she whispered.

"Sleep well." His deep voice coming out of the darkness shivered along her nerves.

For a while, she lay in the darkness fearing that she wouldn't sleep. She knew she was tired following last night's short sleep and all of today's fresh air and activity. She'd had that nap by the stream, though. Maybe if she thought about…

Nadine awoke to a hand on her arm and a large presence hovering over her. She opened her mouth to scream.

Zach's voice stopped her just in time. "It's me."

Disoriented, her gaze shot around. The cabin. The twins. Her heart raced. "What's going on?"

"You were dreaming. Making noise. I didn't want you to wake the boys."

She groaned. Zach sat on the edge of the narrow bed, his hip and thigh warm against hers.

"What—what was I saying?" she asked.

"Mostly 'no,' over and over again."

She covered her face with her hands. Tears burned behind her eyelids. She fought to contain them. It was bad enough that Zach had caught her dreaming. It would be devastating to fall apart in front of him. And what if the boys woke up and heard her crying?

"Do you want to talk about it?" Zach's deep voice, comforting voice rumbled through her.

His hand rested on her shoulder. She drew strength from his warmth. Zach deserved honesty, but dear God it was hard to open up. "I don't know if I can talk about it."

"Do you want to try?"

"Will the boys wake up?"

"They're sound sleep. If we're just talking, they'll be fine."

Which meant she had been very loud. She'd always wondered.

"Does it have to do with the reason you came home to Rodeo?" he prompted.

She flinched. "How did you know?"

"It makes sense. When you left here, you swore you would never come back. You were full of ambition. You were going to set the world on fire."

"How did you know that about me?"

"I knew." She sensed a smile in his voice. So. He had noticed her.

She lay still so she wouldn't dislodge his hand from her shoulder. His touch steadied her.

He continued, "I never thought you'd return voluntarily. You came back a different person. You're caged in. Flat. Not enthusiastic like you used to be."

Oh, dear. She'd wondered how much that showed. She'd thought she'd put on a good face. Zach noticed a lot about her. Maybe the thought should have bothered her, but it didn't. There had always been something deeply decent and caring about Zach...and he'd noticed her. Nadine, of all people.

Her throat was parched. "Is there any ginger ale left?"

"Yeah. I'll get us both some."

She lay on her back with her forearm across her eyes and listened to Zach in the kitchen area. He returned with two plastic cups.

She sat up and swallowed the cold drink in almost one shot. "Thanks. I needed that."

Zach sipped his drink. "So what happened?"

She suppressed a hiccup. "I've never told anyone."

He shifted away from her as though surprised. "Not even your girlfriends? Not even Vy?"

"No one."

"So whatever it was, it was bad. You can't keep that kind of thing, whatever it is, bottled up inside, Nadine. It's making you cry in your sleep. It sounded like you were having a nightmare."

"I was. It was about something that happened. I've never been able to reconcile what was my responsibility and what wasn't. Over a year later, I still don't have answers and the guilt..."

God, she was tired.

Zach set their cups on the floor. He took one of her hands in his. She welcomed the rasp of his calluses against her soft skin. She was coming to like their differences, the contrasts in their characters and in their bodies.

"Start at the beginning," he said.

She told him first about going to school and doing well there, then job hunting for months before finally being hired at the television station and working her way up.

"I was good, Zach. Damned good. Maybe it would have been better if I were lousy at the job. I think I got cocky."

Zach was soothing to talk to, simply by being quiet and patient.

"You're a good listener."

"Yeah." He laughed. "It takes less energy than talking."

She'd noticed before how self-deprecating he was, in a joking way. She liked it.

The urge to tell her secret overwhelmed her. The burden of guilt she'd carried was almost more than she could bear. She had made one fatal error that had killed her career. And that had been the least of the harm done. Far worse had been the damage to her spirit. And to others.

She could lie to Zach and tell him it was nothing. She could fudge the whole sordid story and gloss it over. Or she could tell the truth.

Lying here in as vulnerable a place as she had ever been, she wanted someone to know.

Zach was here and ready to listen.

Here goes. "So I worked my way into a reporting gig. On-air reporting is exciting. You never know what's going to happen when you're live."

Zach's deep, listening stillness encouraged her.

"I'd worked hard to get to that point. There I was,

finally in the city I had always wanted to live in, but I worked so much overtime I could barely enjoy it."

The night was mild and her blanket cozy, but nothing could warm the core of her that had been frozen since that awful night. It had been a year since it happened. It felt like only last week.

"I rose in the ranks, starting with fluff pieces until I moved up to the city hall beat. What I really wanted was to do the tough, hard-hitting stories that would have people sitting up and taking notice of Nadine Campbell."

When she spoke her own name, bitterness spilled into her tone, her former hubris disgusting her.

"I thought a larger network would pick me up if they saw how good I was. So I went after this assignment that all the reporters wanted and I managed to snag it." She had cajoled her boss into giving it to her. "I set out into the worst, grittiest parts of the city. Fortunately, my cameraman was a big guy with tattoos and piercings everywhere. No one would mess with him, so I was safe."

"False security?" Zach asked.

"No. I was safe with Creeper. That was his real name. Nick Creeper." *But others weren't safe from me.* "Anyway, it started as a mini-documentary about homelessness, but that was too tame for me. I wanted to hit hard. I found this young man. A drug addict."

His image would be seared into her memory for the remainder of her life.

Zach made a noise deep in his throat for her to continue.

"Sweet, young James," Nadine said, the boy's name sacrilege on her tongue. How dare she say it aloud? "He was a vulnerable boy."

"Did you like him?"

"Very much. Apart from the official interviews I had

with him, we had great conversations. I thought him intelligent and sensitive. After every interview, I fed him."

"Good of you."

She refused to take praise. She shot back, "It was the least I could do. He was letting me into his life. I followed him around. He was willing to talk for the price of a meal. I interviewed him ruthlessly. Where was he from? Why was he on the streets? What was his background? Where were his parents? Why weren't they helping him?"

Her chest hurt and she rubbed her breastbone. "I was aggressive. Not one speck of his story was any of my business, but he needed the free food."

Still Zach waited, silent and patient. Was that disapproval she felt streaming from him in waves?

One glance told her she was wrong. The disapproval was her guilt reflected inward and eating her up.

"No, it was about more than just the meals. James had a generous spirit." She had genuinely enjoyed spending time with him.

"What happened?" The warmth in Zach's voice eased her pain. Marginally. He hadn't heard the worst of it.

"One night I went to find him, but couldn't. A bunch of the regulars who hung out under this one particular bridge where I usually met him told me they thought he'd climbed up onto the bridge."

She didn't want to tell him the rest, but it was too late to stop now.

"I went up onto the road. James was nowhere. Then someone gasped. I followed his gaze way, way up. James was standing on the girders at the very top of the bridge." She brought her legs to her chest and pressed her forehead to her knees.

That night's terrible dread, and her fear and panic,

flooded her. Oh, James. "I climbed up. Creeper stayed on the ground. To my regret, I didn't call 9-1-1." She rubbed her forehead. "I can't remember…did I think someone else had or did I just want to get the story?"

Zach wrapped his long fingers around her wrist. "You would have thought someone else called."

She jerked her arm from his grasp. "You don't know that," she hissed, then lowered her voice because of the boys sleeping mere feet away. "Don't give me the benefit of the doubt. I don't deserve it. I don't deserve benediction or blessing or grace. You didn't know me then, Zach."

"I know you, Nadine."

"Stop! Listen. I'm not finished." She swiped her arm across her sweaty forehead. When had the cabin become so hot? Her body couldn't decide on a temperature and just stick with it. "I climbed all the way up and stood next to him."

"Weren't you frightened?"

"I was terrified."

She sensed him nodding.

"I asked him what he was doing. I was careful. I thought I was dealing with drug-induced visions or something, and that James didn't know where he was or that he was hanging out at the top of a lethal drop to the river."

She shoved hair back from her forehead.

"He knew. He was lucid, about as aware as I had ever seen him. He told me that he was killing himself. At first, despite the circumstances, I almost didn't believe him. He'd never said a word about being tempted by that kind of thing, you know?"

Zach didn't respond. He just let her hang out with her silence until she became so antsy she had to break it.

"So we talked and out of this young man poured such pain." He'd taken her breath away, telling her things he hadn't shared, going deeper than before. "When I was a teenager, I'd thought I'd been mistreated, but it was nothing compared to what James went through. *Nothing.*"

Zach made a sound of surprise. "What do you mean?"

"James had lived through hell."

"Not that, Nadine. How were you mistreated?"

Damn. She hadn't meant to let that slip. "It doesn't matter."

He grasped her wrist again, his hold gentle but firm. He meant business. He wasn't letting go until he got an answer. "It matters. Tell me."

It was the middle of the night and she'd reached her limit. "I'm exhausted, Zach. I can't do both tonight. Can I just finish telling you about James? Please?"

He eased his hold on her. "Okay."

Thank God. She could only handle so much.

"Anyway." She picked up her story. That one word startled a bitter laugh out of her. *Story.* If only. This was harsh reality. "We talked for a long time while Creeper filmed us from below. I'm ashamed to say it, but I knew this would add depth to the documentary. I poured out what I thought was a whole bunch of wisdom. I thought I was getting through to him. That I was talking him down."

"But only one of you came down whole."

"I came down in one piece, but I haven't felt whole since."

"Tell me."

"James said it was time. Just like that. He smiled, said it was time and dropped off the girder."

The scene played through her mind end over end, too

vivid, too real, too surreal—as it had for nights, weeks, months afterward. As it still did while she slept.

"Just like that, this beautiful young man was gone. One minute there and the next…not. I hadn't thought he would really do it. In my arrogance, I had thought the platitudes I'd been mouthing would save him. No wonder his smile had been so full of pity, not for himself, but for me. I just wasn't getting it. I wasn't getting *him*."

She shivered, cold again.

"They said he wouldn't even have drowned. He would have died the second he hit the water. From that height, it would have been like hitting concrete."

She spoke from the bottom of her heart. "Just before he jumped, he looked so…at peace. Oh, Zach, I want peace, too."

Slowly, as though gentling a skittish horse, Zach reached for her and settled her against his chest. "You can cry if you need to."

"No, I can't. I've tried." She hissed out a breath. "Oh, Zach, I've tried so hard, but there's no release."

"No, I guess not after witnessing something like that."

His voice rumbled against her ear, soothing. She would give anything to *be* soothed, but she couldn't accept it. She had to set him straight. "I didn't witness it, Zach. I caused it. In my self-absorption, I didn't try hard enough to stop him."

"And in your self-absorption now, you're taking responsibility for a choice *he* made. Not you. *Him*." Zach sounded angry.

"But I—"

He urged her away from his chest, his hand firm on her cheek so he could meet her eye in the dim light of a full moon beyond the window above her bed.

"Who do you think you are?" he asked. "God?"

She gasped. "Don't be cruel."

"I'm not. I'm giving you a solid dose of reality. *James* made a choice. You didn't make it for him one way or the other."

"How do you know that?"

"Did you go up there with him or did you follow him up there?"

"I told you. He was already up there and I went once I realized where he was."

"He was already up there because he'd made his decision. You *might* have been able to talk him down, but it sounds like his mind was made up."

She thought hard, trying to separate her emotions from what had actually happened that night.

"Was that smile of his really sad because of you?" Zach asked. "Or were you maybe not the center of his attention in that moment?"

She tried to study the situation as objectively as she could. "I don't know." She'd been racked with guilt for too long to be able to just let it go.

"How did you feel about being up so high? High enough that the water would have been concrete if you had fallen?"

"I already told you. I was terrified."

"You went up there even though you were frightened?"

"The story, Zach. I was after the story."

"I don't know, Nadine."

"I do."

"Let's leave it for now."

What did *for now* mean? That he thought he could convince her otherwise? Never.

"It took courage to tell me this, Nadine. Thank you."

After a gentle kiss on her forehead, he urged her under the blankets.

"Let's get back to sleep," Zach said. "Those boys will be up early. Trust me on this."

Back to the mundane and the normal, thank goodness. Yes. She needed normal life, not painful memories, not the exhaustion of culpability.

Zach had been right to get her to talk. She didn't agree with his conclusions, but she did feel better. The weight she carried could now be measured in pounds instead of tons.

Drained, she closed her eyes. She touched her forehead where Zach's lips had been. So sweet. She slept.

Chapter Six

Nadine had given Zach a gift last night, a glimpse into her soul.

Her story had saddened, alarmed and worried him. She took too much responsibility and he didn't know how to ease it for her.

What he had heard, but he didn't think Nadine yet realized, was that she had truly cared more for James than for her story.

"Hey," she said to the boys as they loaded up the truck to drive back to the ranch house. "What about the mystery? Wasn't there supposed to be a clue here for me?"

Was it Zach's imagination, or did she seem lighter this morning, more like her old self? That would be too much recovery too soon, he knew, but her smile glowed in the morning sun. And it dazzled him. He would treasure the memory of those moments alone with her while she'd talked last night.

The loading of leftover food and supplies abandoned, the boys ran into the cabin, followed by Nadine.

Zach stood in the doorway to watch. Sunlight streamed through the window over Nadine's bed, or what he would always think of now as her bed.

Ryan pointed to a small box on the high mantel.

"Can you get that down?" Aiden asked for the small

cedar chest Zach had made as a teenager, his attempt at carpentry work. He'd done a good enough job, but he would never make his living at it.

Nadine took it down.

"Open it!" Ryan ordered.

She did.

Zach didn't know what was inside. In fact, he had no idea what the boys had planned. Ryan and Aiden were being unusually secretive about this whole mystery business. They giggled a lot about it. They liked Nadine.

So did he.

More than ever, especially after last night's emotional intimacy, he wanted her in his life. Yes, she had made a big mistake, but not what she had thought. Her mistake had been in believing she could make a difference in that young man's life.

Sure, she had wanted the story, but she had also tried to talk him down. It wasn't her fault that James had made up his mind long before Nadine arrived on the scene.

She'd felt true affection for James and his death had devastated her.

"What does this mean?" she asked. She held a tiny china teacup from an old children's play tea set.

Where on earth had the boys found it? Magpies, the pair of them. It could have come from anywhere or anyone. The twins collected strange things and the townspeople often set small treasures aside for them. Zach had certainly never seen this tiny cup before.

Nadine read aloud from the note in her hand. "Roses are red, violets are blue, company is good, we like you, too."

What did it mean and what did the boys have in mind? As far as Zach could tell, none of the clues so far had anything to do with a mystery and everything to do with getting Nadine back out here to the ranch. Were they inviting her to tea? If so, fine with him. The more often she came out here the better.

This had to be the most subtle of seductions in all of history. Did she even know she was being courted? It seemed the boys were doing more of his courting for him than Zach was.

Yesterday, there had been that moment looking out over his slice of Montana together when she seemed to be coming around to liking the land.

Next step in the process was getting her out here again and finding out for certain whether she could like the ranch, and him, enough to live here.

"Well, I have to admit I'm stumped," Nadine said. "Will you guys give me a hint?"

"We saw on that baking show that making tea parties is really pretty," Aiden said.

What baking show? What were Rick and the boys watching while Zach was out working?

"You're a girl. Do you like tea parties?" Ryan asked her.

Nadine laughed. "I like tea. I like parties. I like baked goods. So I guess the answer is yes. I like tea parties, I think. I've never been to one."

"Come to ours!"

"We'll make you one."

"When?" she asked, glancing at Zach.

Ryan said, "Tomorrow afternoon at two o'clock."

Aiden glanced at Zach, too. "Is that okay, Dad? Is it the right time for a tea party?"

He shrugged. "As good a time as any. Do you boys know what's involved in a tea party?"

"We'll find out!"

Nadine would have to combine it with work. "I'm

coming to interview your father again. We'll work it around that." Nadine turned to Zach. "Do you mind?"

"Not at all." How could he? His boys were doing a great job of getting Nadine back out here.

"What should I do with this?" she asked, holding up the tiny teacup.

"Keep it," Aiden said. "It's a present from us."

"I'll treasure it." Nadine slipped it into the same purse pocket she'd tucked the little yellow Monopoly house into yesterday.

Zach thought she might mean exactly what she had said.

"Come on, Dad! We have to go home so Pop can take us grocery shopping."

"We need to buy stuff," Aiden said. He paused to peer up at his father. "What kind of stuff?"

"Did Pop watch the baking show with you? The one about tea parties?"

They bobbed their small, identical heads in the affirmative.

"Good," Zach said. "He can advise you." What Zach knew about putting on tea parties could fit into, well, a teaspoon.

They finished loading the truck and drove back to the house. After hugging Nadine and grabbing a couple of lighter things to carry inside, the boys ran off.

"How about if we ride out after the tea party tomorrow? As part of your research for the article? Remember I said there's something I have to show you on the other side of the mountain?"

She nodded. "That will allow me to work in the office in the morning. I'd like to dress up for the tea party, though, for the boys' sake. I think they'd really like that.

They might expect me to play a part, if you know what I mean. Who knows what they saw on that TV show."

"Could you bring a change of clothes for riding?"

"Yes, I can do that."

Zach walked her to her car. She got in and opened the driver's window. Zach rested his forearms on the window and leaned close. "Thanks for all you're doing for my sons. I know this has nothing to do with the article. I appreciate it."

"Zach…" She looked uncomfortable. "About last night…" When he would have interrupted, she raised one hand to stop him.

"I can't tell you how much it meant to me to be able to tell my story." She gripped the steering wheel. She had a lot of emotion wrapped up in that New York business. "As a journalist, I should be more articulate than this, but…thank you."

"It was my pleasure." What else could he say? That encapsulated it all. "The whole day yesterday and the evening and the talk during the night were my pleasure."

She smiled. Funny how one smile could brighten an already brilliant day. "Those boys are good for me right now, Zach. They lighten my days. It's great to spend time with them, so don't think I'm doing you a favor. The benefits are all mine."

With that, she drove away.

And me? Zach thought. *Do I lighten your days? Am I good for you, too?*

He watched until her car was a pinprick on the highway, then went off to live his everyday life, hoping that maybe, just maybe, he might be able to persuade her to care for him as much as his boys.

AT HOME, Nadine swabbed the old makeup from her face, washed and showered, and reapplied fresh makeup.
She unpacked her bag and washed her dirty clothes right away. Twenty minutes later, her jeans were in the dryer and her backpack on its shelf in the closet and her apartment as neat as a pin.

At her home computer, she wrote about the land that Zach had shown to her and her impressions about it, the beauty of it, and how she began to see, just briefly, some of what Zach saw.

The article was coming along more slowly than usual, but she was spending a lot of time at the ranch. Too much time.

Funny, she remembered on her one visit in high school how much she had disliked it. At the moment, she couldn't remember why.

The upside was that she was getting glimpses into Zach she couldn't possibly get with simple interviews.

It was going to be a good article.

Thinking about Lee's purpose, she went online to look up the death so many years ago, but found only the news from the *Rodeo Wrangler* that she'd already read.

She emailed Lee downstairs to bring him up to date on the article.

Going through her many emails, she added more announcements to her columns.

She sat on the sofa, the silence weighing on her instead of soothing her. What a contrast between this and the night spent with the boys. And with Zach.

Zach was… Well, she didn't know what she thought of Zach. He'd always been handsome. Hell, gorgeous, in his taciturn, intense way. But there was tenderness and affection inside of him that was even more attractive than the lean, rugged exterior.

She might worry about the affection growing inside of her if it wasn't tempered with common sense. She had no desire to live on a ranch. He had two children. She was *not* up to starting anything that might involve a ready-made family. And weren't those kinds of thoughts more than a little premature? All she had done was to have a nice evening with him and his boys.

And share her innermost, darkest secret with the man in the middle of the night. *Don't forget that important detail, Nadine.*

Speaking of which, how odd that she'd shared with him and not with her friends. It felt disloyal.

Well, that was easy enough to fix, wasn't it? In just— she checked her watch—half an hour, she was meeting her friends at Honey's bar for their weekly fair revival update before the bar opened for the day.

But where did this new connection with Zach leave her with the *Rodeo Wrangler* story and the Brandts' secret? What about that awful suspicion she had about Zach's family?

She could talk to Zach when she rode out with him, to try to determine whether he knew anything about his grandparents.

Her stomach did a triple axel. After last night's midnight confession with Zach, how could she still consider betraying him?

She stared around her apartment. After all of her work in über-expensive New York City, after all of the commitment to her career and the overtime worked, she had little to show for it. She didn't own much.

She needed her job.

Ruthlessly, she separated her feelings into compartments, building solid walls between them. One thing at a time.

First, she would talk to her friends.

In the morning, she planned to do more research downstairs into dates of birth. When was Rick's birthday? How soon after Judith's marriage to Richard? Tomorrow afternoon, she would enjoy her tea party with those two charming little boys. Only later would she talk to Zach and maybe ruin his life and hers yet again.

First things first.

What she was about to do was hard, hard, hard. What would her friends think of her?

Twenty minutes later, she arrived at Honey's Place, the first of the committee to arrive. Chet was already there, prepping food for the day. He was a big, tattooed, intimidating guy, and everyone who patronized the popular bar loved him.

"Honey said she'll be here in a minute," he said.

Nadine sat at the table they usually occupied for their weekly meetings and waited.

A minute later, Max entered the bar in her usual loose old jeans and denim shirt. Just once, Nadine wished Max would let her take her shopping.

Following on Max's heels was Vy and then Honey. Rachel entered with her baby, Beth, on her shoulder.

Last to arrive was Samantha.

After the usual catching up chitchat, Honey called the meeting to order. "How is everyone doing? Samantha, do you want to start with how things look with our books?"

"Oh!" Nadine said. "That reminds me." From her purse, she pulled the check Vy had given her. "Sam sent along two thousand dollars for advertising."

Samantha took it from her. "That's so generous, Vy. Thank Sam for us."

"Already done." A satisfied grin lit her face and everyone knew exactly what form her gratitude had taken. Quirked eyebrows and smiles flew around the table.

The only one who looked awkward was Max.

Samantha gave an account of the fair's costs that brought everyone down to earth. They were spending so much and not one of them could afford to be left in debt.

"Let's move on." Honey turned to Rachel. "The rides look incredible. You did an outstanding job refurbishing them."

Rachel tucked her sleeping daughter against her chest. "Thanks, Honey. I had a good time doing it. I had to get rid of a couple of ancient classics that just couldn't be salvaged well enough to be safe. I think there will still be enough rides left to satisfy the crowds, though."

"I see by the mechanic's fees that you got the rest checked out," Samantha said.

"Yes. Every ride passed inspection."

"Hope we get crowds," Max said. "We're going to need them."

"How are the rodeo plans going?" Honey asked her.

"We're going to keep most of the standard rodeo events, but I'm still working to find a way to substitute something else for the bull riding," Max said.

"What about Sam's suggestion of a polo match?" Vy asked.

"He and I have been discussing it. I'll let everyone know whenever I finalize things."

Honey frowned. "It's only a month away."

"I know," Max snapped. What on earth? She pulled back quickly. "Sorry. I shouldn't use that tone. I'll pull it together, everyone. Don't worry. I have to go."

With that, Max did what she always did: she stood abruptly to leave.

"I'd better get this little one home to bed." Rachel stood as well.

Nadine ignored the flutters of nerves in her stomach and said, "Um, could I have everyone's attention? Just for a minute before you leave?"

If she left the telling of her secret for another week, her nerves would kill her…and maybe she would take the coward's way out and never share.

Alerted by her tone, they sat back down.

Panicking, Nadine turned to Honey. "We forgot to discuss food and beverages."

Honey waved her hand. "I have it under control."

She looked closely at Nadine. "How are you doing?" she asked.

"Me?" Nadine started to outline all of the promotion she'd done all summer, but her voice shook.

Honey touched her hand. "I don't mean that. I mean you. How are *you* doing?"

"I'm good. Of course."

"Something's up." Pointedly, Honey looked around at the other women.

Nadine rested her forehead on her hand. "God, I don't know how…"

"I can always tell when there's something bothering you." Nadine avoided Honey's probing gaze, but her friend pressed on. "Usually you become too cool and collected, even more than usual, as if your life depended on maintaining control. Right now, though, you seem like a nervous wreck. Spill," Honey ordered.

"This is a business meeting. I don't know why I thought it was appropriate to—"

"Nadine," Rachel said, her warm voice flowing over her. "We are your friends. You are troubled about something. We're here together now. Please talk to us."

"I haven't sorted it all out. My mind is such a jumble. I have so much to tell you all. Something happened yesterday that had me thinking of my mom."

Whoa. Where had *that* come from? It wasn't at all what she had wanted to share today.

"What happened?" Max asked.

Too late to take it back now.

"You know I'm writing an article about Zach's painting, right? I've gone out there a few times this week. His sons invited me out for a sleepover in a cabin on their property."

"How sweet." Rachel liked anything to do with children.

"It really was. They are delightful boys. Sometimes I can even tell them apart." Her grin felt slightly sickly. "Anyway, I watched Zach with his sons. He's an amazing father. Just wonderful. It brought back memories of my mom, who was also amazing. I thought about what my life might have been like if she hadn't died. I thought about *her*, which I haven't done in a long time."

"What about her?" Max asked, leaning toward Nadine in a show of support. "What did seeing Zach with his children bring up?"

"Did I ever tell you she was an unwed mother?"

"No, but I'm not surprised." Honey took one of Nadine's hands into her own.

"Why not?"

"You haven't shared much about your background, but you have always been sad. There's a reason we all became friends, and it seems to be that we all have something in our backgrounds that hurt us and make us sympathetic to each other."

"We really do get each other, don't we?" Vy stated.

"Yes, we sure do." Honey smiled.

"For me," Nadine said, "it was my parents' deaths when I was a child."

"Wait," Samantha interjected. "*Parents?* But you just said your mom was unwed."

"She was. She met my stepdad soon after giving birth to me and they got married. He took me on as his own. I never thought of him as my stepfather. He was my father, pure and simple."

Rachel took her other hand in hers. "That's lovely, Nadine."

"So why was your mom's pregnancy with you a problem?" Max asked. "It sounds like things worked out for her and your dad. Even close to thirty years ago, it was no longer a taboo to be unwed and pregnant."

"It wasn't a problem for her or my dad, but it was for my aunt," Nadine recalled.

"Denise?" Max frowned. "Why would it be a problem for her?"

"She often referred to how bad my mom had been to do that."

"Hmm," Honey said. "Too bad. I had her pegged as a nice lady."

"She wasn't. Max, you're right that it was no big deal that my mom got pregnant. What hurt was her death and then having to live with Denise, who didn't approve of my mom."

"I wish I'd known what Denise was like," Max said. "I would have given her a piece of my mind."

If Nadine weren't so sad, she would laugh. Max would have confronted Aunt Denise for her. Nadine sighed and rested her chin in her hands. "Everything's coming up lately."

"Does it have anything to do with interviewing Zach?" Honey asked.

"Sort of. I'm investigating an event in his family's past and it's stirring feelings in me. I haven't even found anything that bad yet, and already I feel sad."

"You look tired." Samantha squeezed her shoulder. "You need to get a good night's sleep."

"I do. Thanks for listening."

"No problem. You know we're always here for you. All of us are."

Nadine stood and picked up her purse. Maybe that was enough for today. She really was tired. She started to leave but Honey said, "You know you can also tell us why you decided to come home."

Staggered, Nadine hung her head. She'd almost escaped without getting into it.

"We know you weren't homesick. You were living your dream. We've never pushed you, but if you're feeling emotional lately, maybe it would help to get it off your chest." Honey stood and hugged her. "If you need a friend, I'm here."

Nadine leaned into her embrace. "I know. Thank you."

She'd tried so hard to suppress everything since returning home, but now Zach and his curiosity were forcing her to look at emotions and memories.

Last night had been good for her. She'd released some of her burden and Zach hadn't judged her.

She looked at her friends and suddenly wanted it all out in the open. Secrets could fester and damage you from within.

It was time.

Nadine opened her mouth to speak.

She told her friends what she had already shared with Zach, and because she had told him about it, it was easier to tell her friends. And wasn't that strange? If anything it should be easier because they were her best friends, the dearest people to her on this earth. Her *family* in the purest sense of the word.

But she had shared this devastating story with Zach first. What did that say about her? About Zach? About… everything?

When she finished, she held her breath, afraid to look at the women around the table and see disappointment or worse, revulsion, in their eyes.

Strong-willed, opinionated Vy responded exactly how Nadine would have guessed, with sympathy but also with anger. "You should have told us. We're here for each other through thick and thin, Nadine."

Yes, she knew that, but James's suicide had been awful. Despite talking to Zach last night, she still hadn't sorted out what had been her responsibility and what hadn't. "Thanks, Vy. I guess I thought I could handle it on my own."

"You thought wrong."

Vy was beyond blunt. Nadine took no offense. She knew it came from love. Vy pointed at Nadine. "You come to us next time something goes wrong in your life. We'll always be here."

She got the same reaction from every other woman seated at the table and her eyes filled with tears. Oh, these amazing, dependable, loving women.

"I've spent enough time healing in Rodeo, but I don't know what comes next in my life. I'm just surviving. Subsisting."

"Healing?" Vy asked. "I don't think so. You've been hiding out."

"Yes. I guess you're right."

"Why confess this today? Now?" Rachel covered Nadine's hand with her own. Nadine struggled to come up with an adequate reply.

"What has changed lately?" Vy pressed. "You haven't said a thing for a full year, then all of a sudden you spill the whole story. You said you were upset about your mother."

Again, Nadine hesitated to respond.

"Does this have anything to do with Zach?" Honey asked. "Apart from how great he is as a father?"

She hated to tell. But she'd already come this far. "Since James died, I've had nightmares."

"Of course you have," Max said. What had happened in her past? Nadine wondered, that there was so much understanding in her eyes.

"I had one last night while I was staying in the cabin," Nadine continued. "Zach comforted me."

Vy perked up. "Comforted? How?"

Nadine sent her a suppressing frown. "His two boys were in the cabin with us."

"Damn."

Nadine burst into laughter. "Vy, you are irrepressible."

Her friend grinned. "Damned straight." She sobered. "What did Zach do?"

"He listened and I just…opened up to him. I told him the whole thing. This morning it felt disloyal to have told him but none of you."

Vy patted her arm. "I'm just glad you finally opened up to us." She stood. "But you still haven't answered our question. Do all of these revelations have anything to do with Zach that's deeper than him simply being in the right place at the right time?"

"Of course not."

"Hmm," was all Vy said before she stood to leave.

"I have to agree with Vy," Rachel said.

"Agree with her? All she said was 'hmm.'"

Honey grinned. "Exactly. Suspicious timing."

Nadine couldn't handle much more right now. She was hitting a wall. "I need to go lie down for a while."

"Okay. Thank you, Nadine, for sharing." Rachel hugged her and held on hard for a moment.

Everyone else hugged her before she left. Still friends after all of these years, and after her shame-filled confession. There were no better people on earth.

Back in her apartment, she lay down on her bed fully dressed and fell asleep right away.

THE NEXT MORNING, Nadine went online to check public records. She looked through more microfiches in the office.

Lee asked what she was working on.

"The article. I'm going back through Brandt history."

"Good." Lee seemed to have relaxed since she'd agreed to do the article his way.

She found what she was looking for. Rick Brandt was born eight months after Richard and Judith's wedding and he was a good weight. Not a preemie.

Judith had been pregnant before they married.

For the rest of the morning, she copy edited Lee's articles. He did the same for her announcement and news columns.

"I'm heading back out to interview Zach again."

Lee nodded and kept working when she left.
After a light lunch, she dressed with care, putting on a pink top with a flared, floral skirt. She cinched the waist with a wide white leather belt. On her feet, she wore pink high heels.

She packed a bag with her jeans and a T-shirt and drove out to the ranch.

Someone had lined the steps of the veranda with pots of hot pink geraniums. A wreath of leaves and flowers had been hung on the screen door. Someone had visited the garden center. A sisal welcome mat had been placed on the floor in front of the door.

Oh, my-y-y-y, they'd gone all out. For her.

It had been years since anyone had taken the time to do something just for her. Warmed through, she knocked on the screen door.

Noise erupted from inside the house and the boys ran down the hallway toward her. How could two small boys make such a racket?

Zach's voice from somewhere inside said, "Boys, calm down."

They didn't and Nadine smiled. She liked that they were excited about seeing her.

"You look pretty!"

An exclamation. That had to be Ryan. "Thank you, Ryan. I wanted to look special for your party."

"You do," Aiden answered solemnly and she smiled.

They led her down the hallway. The first thing she noticed was the music. Classical music drifted from a room on the left. In the dining room, a room she hadn't seen before today, the table had been set with a white tablecloth and china with roses on it.

"It used to belong to my mother," Zach said from behind her.

She turned to him. He wore a white button-down shirt with black jeans, the white stark against his tanned skin and dark hair. Her breath caught in her throat. She rarely saw him in anything other than a T-shirt and faded blue jeans.

He looked good. Damned good.

She swallowed and looked back at the table, anything to distract herself from Zach's pure male beauty. He radiated masculinity and virility.

Why hadn't she noticed that before today? Well. She had, but she'd ignored it. Standing beside him in the dining room, with heat radiating from his gorgeous body, she couldn't ignore the man. Not even for a second.

"We made the table pretty for you!"

"It's beautiful, Ryan. Look at the embroidery on the tablecloth."

"We picked out the flowers all by ourselves," Aiden said quietly. A vase full of flowers graced the center of the table.

"I love the mix of pink roses with white daisies." Nadine fingered the down of one rose petal.

"I put the sunflower in there." Ryan pointed to one oversize yellow sunflower among the more subtle blooms. The effect was a bit jarring, but it was the loveliest bouquet she'd ever seen.

Zach pulled out the chair at one end of the table and seated himself at the other. Oh, dear. She was going to have to look at him for at least the next hour.

The boys sat on either side of the table.

"No Rick?" Nadine asked.

"He's in town having a beer with his buddies," Zach said. "Taking advantage of a rare afternoon off."

Aiden patted her hand, every bit as though she had said she was feeling lonely without the man. "He'll come back before you go out riding with Dad. You'll still see him."

She hid a smile behind her other hand.

At the other end of the table, Zach rubbed the back of his neck, his bicep flexing against his rolled up sleeve.

Nadine stared, not certain she'd ever seen anything more masculine than Zach's arm.

Whoa, Nadine. Pull yourself together. You do not

find Zach that attractive. You're here to pay attention to the boys.

But Zach drew her eye. He leaned his elbow on the table and turned his face away. It looked like he was struggling not to smile at Aiden's earnest concern, too.

"We already made the tea," Ryan said. "It's ready! Dad said it was okay because you're always punktal."

Nadine frowned.

"Punc-tu-al," Zach and Aiden both said at the same time.

"That's what I said."

Again, Zach struggled not to laugh. So did Nadine. These boys were inching further and further into her heart, crumbling defenses she'd built years ago.

Zach stood, walked around the table to her side and poured tea into a china cup decorated with red roses and gilt edges.

So carefully it looked like a pantomime, Ryan handed her a plate of crustless sandwiches. She took one that looked like egg salad and another that had sliced cucumbers and butter.

The plate went around the table. The boys each took a bite of a cucumber sandwich, then made identical faces of distaste.

"That lady lied!" Ryan said.

"Who?" Zach asked.

"The lady on the baking show said these would be good," Aiden said. "They're not. They just taste like vegetables inside of bread."

"Fill up on the egg salad," Zach suggested. "Nadine and I can eat the cuke sandwiches."

"Are you sure?" Aiden asked.

"Positive," Nadine assured him. "I like cucumbers."

Ryan looked at her as though he couldn't understand why anyone would, but she just shrugged.

"There's no accounting for taste, Ryan," Zach said.

"I guess not."

The twins stuffed egg salad sandwiches into their mouths as though they were starving.

"Boys, slow down," Zach said. "What's the rush?"

"Cake, Dad!"

"Ah," Zach said, as though that explained everything. He caught Nadine's eye. "There's dessert in the kitchen."

In addition to cake, dessert turned out to be home-made lemon tarts—homemade by Vy at the diner, Nadine guessed—and sugar cookies so poorly decorated they had to have been made right here. The twins had gone a little heavy on the multicolored sprinkles.

The cake was really a loaf, a pretty confection that looked like lemon with a sugar and lemon glaze. Someone had decorated it with candied violets.

Nadine stared. "Who made that?"

Zach, rock solid and confident, blushed for the third time this week. "I did," he mumbled.

"You? But it's so…"

"Pretty!" Ryan said. "Yeah!"

"Dad asked at the bakery how to decorate a cake for a lady and the baker gave him flowers to put on top."

"They're made of candy!"

"No, Ryan," Zach said, his neck still flushed. "They're not candy. They're candied. There's a difference."

"What's the difference, Dad?"

"Candy is made out of sugar, but these are real flowers that have been coated with sugar."

Ryan studied him dubiously.

Nadine studied Zach, too, but he refused to meet her eye.

So it wasn't just the twins who had put effort into making her a lovely tea party. Zach had not only baked a loaf, but he'd also cared enough to find out how to make it look attractive. Another defense around her heart crumbled.

Oh, she had to be careful. She was not worthy of the man.

Denise had drummed into her that she was not worthy of any man.

Aiden watched her solemnly. For his sake, she brightened, setting aside every worry and putting her heart into enjoying what these three boys had done for her.

Zach's loaf was delicious, but the twins' cookies were too sweet for her taste. She ate a couple, and chased them down with a lemon tart and two more cups of tea.

As she took another sip of the warm, milky drink, a painting off to the side caught her attention. From the passion in the brushstrokes, Nadine knew it had to be one of Zach's. The rural image hadn't been rendered as a photograph. Brilliant colors slashed the canvas across a backdrop of such detailed subtly it would take a good hour of study to *see* everything.

But it wasn't local scenery.

Before she could ask, he said, "China."

"It's absolutely stunning."

"Thank you."

"Someday I would love to see all the paintings from your travels."

A slow smile built on his well-defined lips. It took her breath away. Again that elbow made its appearance on the table, a breach of manners, yes, but the sight of his strong, tanned forearm set a fire burning low in Nadine's belly.

Aiden asked, "Was it a good tea party?"

Drawing her attention firmly away from Zach, she leaned back and said, "That was amazing. You sure know how to make a fabulous tea party."

The boys' grins were so broad they looked like their faces could crack.

At that moment, Rick walked in. "How was it?"

"The best! We did good, Pop!"

"I'm not at all surprised. Remember what your dad is always telling you?"

"Effort pays off!"

"That's right, Ryan."

"The cucumbers were yucky," Aiden said, "but everything else was great. Want a cookie, Pop?"

"Maybe after I've digested my beer a bit."

Zach stood. "Let's go, Nadine. I'll saddle the horses while you get changed."

"Wait!"

"What is it, Ryan?" Zach asked.

"We have another clue." Aiden retrieved a small gift bag from the sideboard. It had a torn sticker on it where the top had been folded down. The boys were reusing an old bag. She didn't mind.

She smiled and looked inside. There at the bottom sat a tiny figurine of a cat curled into a ball and sleeping.

"There's no note?" she asked. "No clue?"

"We didn't have time to write one."

"What does this mean?"

"It means you have to come back to see the kittens in the barn."

Nadine looked at Zach. A *very* satisfied smile lit his face. What was that about?

"You should come back and see the kittens," he said.

"Okay."

After promising the boys she'd visit the kittens with

them after their ride, she headed to the bathroom to change. By the time Nadine was ready, so were the horses.

Zach stood in the yard waiting.

They mounted and headed out.

ZACH HAD ENJOYED the tea party. Or would have, if he could have stopped staring at Nadine.

Hadn't he heard someone say that redheads shouldn't wear pink? They'd forgotten to tell Nadine. It was a dumb rule, in his opinion. Pink looked magnificent on her. Her outfit had been colorful and striking, and she was so beautiful in her animated chatter with his sons that it had hurt him to look at her.

He wanted to capture that vivacity and bottle it to keep on his bedside table through long, cold winter nights. Since coming home, she had been a muted version of herself, but somehow his boys were drawing her out of her shell, and she was a wonderful sight to behold.

Zach stared across the land. Clouds formed on the horizon. Sunrise had been beautiful, painting the land deep red.

Red sky at night, sailor's delight, Dad had said over a quiet breakfast with the boys. *Red sky at morning, sailor's warning.* Dad's homespun wisdom had proven to be surprisingly accurate over the years.

There was weather coming in, which left Zach with a decision to make. To ride out? Not to ride out?

He wanted her to see what Tommy Broome was doing to the land on the far edge of the Brandt ranch. If she wanted to understand Zach for her article, Nadine needed to learn how much it tore him apart to see the land abused.

He squinted past sunshine to those clouds in the distance. They were far enough away, he decided. Besides, a little rain never hurt anyone.

He helped Nadine into the saddle. She settled in. He led her out slowly, for him at any rate. He'd been pretty well born in the saddle. He could ride at any pace, but this felt glacial.

"You okay?" he tossed over his shoulder.

"I'm good, Zach."

"We're going to be riding a lot farther than we did with the boys the other day. Let me know if it becomes uncomfortable."

"So far, so good. Thanks."

"You want to come up beside me and we'll do more of that interview?"

"Double duty. Good idea. Stop for a minute."

She got out her recorder and turned it on.

They continued their gentle ride. Zach should have taken Paintbrush out for a good brisk run first. He stirred restively beneath him, wanting to gallop, not plod.

Nadine started in on the same line of questioning from the other day. If Zach didn't give in, she was just going to keep asking.

He sighed and did his best to articulate the incomprehensible. Why did he paint? As hard as it was for him to explain, he found as he made an attempt that he liked talking to Nadine about his painting.

The difference between this interview and the first was that he'd spent more time with her. At the moment, with sincere interest on her face, she wasn't Nadine the reporter, just the woman he knew and liked.

Becoming aware of cooler air, he glanced up. His mountain loomed closer. Unfortunately, so did the rain clouds.

"Aw, hell," he said. He'd gotten lost in talking and had forgotten to keep track of the weather.

"What?"

"That." He pointed to the darkening sky in the not-too-far distance. Sky met earth in a blue-black haze. "That's a wall of rain heading this way."

He spun his horse. Too far to go back—not for him and Paintbrush, but for Nadine and Butter. He steered forward again. "It's closer to go to the cabin. We can't outride it, but we'll do our best to not get caught for long."

She nodded, but fear lurked in her green eyes.

He squeezed her hands on the reins to reassure her. "It's only rain. It won't hurt us. Ride."

He spurred his horse forward and heard Butter follow. Despite his words, he had misgivings. Rain was fine, but not lightning. No one wanted to get caught on the prairie in an electrical storm.

He'd put Nadine on a gentle mare and the animal had stamina, but she didn't have the speed needed to beat this storm. He heard Nadine urge her on and hung back to stay with them, even though Paintbrush wanted to race.

They were still a half-mile or so from the cabin when light and darkness collided in a violent crash of thunder and lightning almost on top of them.

The air smelled metallic.

Zach held Paintbrush under control while he lunged for Butter's reins. Wild-eyed, Butter struggled to turn back. Without experience, Nadine couldn't control her.

Zach grabbed her reins, held tight, spurred on Paintbrush and rode for the cabin.

A wall of cold, thick rain hit hard.

Chapter Seven

By the time they made it to the cabin, they were soaked to the skin. They dismounted in mud.

"Get inside," Zach shouted above the din of pounding rain. "I'll take care of the horses."

"No. I'll help."

If rain hadn't made opening his eyes difficult, Zach would have rolled them. Trust Nadine to not follow orders. On the other hand, between the two of them they got the job done twice as quickly.

With the horses dry, fed and tucked into the small shed expressly built for sheltering horses, they ran for the cabin.

Zach slammed the door behind them. He knelt by the hearth and put a dry match to the kindling already laid out. It took only a moment to get the fire going.

He stood and turned around just in time to see Nadine lean back and squeeze water out of her thick hair.

Her white T-shirt had gone transparent, outlining her full breasts and tight, hard nipples.

She shot him a look and evidently read the shock on his face. He stared at her chest. He couldn't help himself.

She glanced down at herself and yelped. "Oh." She crossed her arms over her breasts and Zach could have wept.

He spun away, remembering all his unformed teenage longings that had matured into pure, adult lust.

God, she was pretty.

The old armoire on the far side of the fireplace, cheap veneer peeling, held spare dry clothes. He yanked open the door. Pulling out a thick flannel shirt, he thrust it behind him without turning. "Put this on."

"Thanks." She took it from him and a second later said, "You can look now."

He did. She was covered, but she'd put the flannel on over her wet shirt. "Not good enough, Nadine. You need to get out of the wet clothes before you put on the dry." Surely she knew that?

By her sheepish expression, she did. "It's just…"

"Just?"

"I won't have any underwear on then. *Everything* got wet."

As much as the thought of her without her bra and panties should have set his libido in flames, he tamped it down to concentrate on practical stuff.

"Take off everything and hang it in front of the fireplace." If he sounded impatient, it was only because he fought an internal battle. "I'm going to step outside to call Rick and tell him where we are. Get changed while I'm gone. There are more clothes in the cupboard. Take what you need."

Zach grabbed a couple of buckets and stepped back out into the rain, his soaked jeans hanging heavy and low on his hips.

He set the buckets out to collect rain water for washing and cleaning dishes.

Under the lip of the shed, he called Rick and assured him they were fine. When he returned to the cabin he found Nadine dressed in old jeans and the oversize flannel shirt. Her wet shirt and pants hung on the backs of a couple of ancient ladder-back chairs turned to face the fire.

"Good," he said. "You'll warm more quickly that way."

From the armoire, he pulled out a shirt and old pants for himself. "Can you turn around for a minute? Actually, check out the pantry and see what's in there."

He heard her rummaging.

"There are a lot of canned goods here."

"Yep." He finished changing and walked up beside her to check. "Someone's been up restocking lately." He strode to the fridge and checked the freezer. He pulled out a loaf of rye bread.

"My foreman, Rafe, likes corned beef sandwiches." He pulled the vacuum-packed meat out of the freezer and covered it with cold water. "It'll thaw quickly."

"There's plenty of mustard in the fridge," Nadine said. "Hey, dill pickles, remember? These'll be great sandwiches." She loaded the counter with sandwich fixings. "That rain was cold. I'm going to boil water for tea or coffee. Which would you prefer?"

"Coffee."

"There's only instant."

"Doesn't bother me."

Nadine shuddered and said, "No, thanks. Not for me."

"Fussy?"

"Instant?"

Zach laughed and turned away. "When you've been out working on the land hard and get stuck up here in bad weather, *anything* tastes good."

"I'll have to take your word for it. I'm going to make myself a cup of tea."

Zach spread his damp boxers on the stone hearth beside Nadine's baby blue scrap of panties and her bra. His gaze skittered away from those. On a couple of hooks on either side of the mantel, he hung his jeans and T-shirt. Crouching, he built up the fire.

A yelp from Nadine had him spinning around. "Did you burn yourself?"

"No. It's that." She pointed to the wall. Above the sink hung an old mirror. Nadine stared at herself.

"What's wrong?" Zach moved up behind her.

"Don't look at me," she said.

Zach couldn't hold back a laugh. She wasn't making sense. "You made a noise that caught my attention and then pointed to the mirror. How could I not look? And why not?"

"My makeup is a mess."

"We just got rained on. What do you expect?"

"I have raccoon eyes."

"I'm not sure we have tissues up here."

"I do in my purse."

"So use them."

"But then I'll have no makeup on."

Zach scratched his head. "Are you saying you'd rather have raccoon eyes than no makeup at all?"

She bit her bottom lip. "I'm not sure."

"Let me make the decision for you. Take it off." He got her purse from the floor by the door and brought it to her. "Here. It's running down your cheeks now."

She broke a speed record getting to the mirror again. "Oh, God."

"It's not the end of the world, Nadine."

When she didn't answer, he took a closer look at her. She was truly upset. "Is it?"

"Is it what?" Her voice sounded thick, like maybe she was just this side of giving in to tears.

"Is it the end of the world if you have to take off your makeup?"

She rummaged in her purse without meeting his eye and mumbled something.

"I beg your pardon?" he asked.

"No one has seen me without makeup since I left town, okay?"

Zach stared. "Am I getting this right? In eight years— or more, was it—not one person has seen you without makeup?"

She looked shattered. Why? How was this bad? It was a small thing. Trivial.

Not to her, Zach. Tread lightly here.

"Talk to me."

"Let me remove this first." Distress undercut what he had thought was merely petulance. Nadine was truly, deeply upset.

NADINE SEARCHED IN her bag until she found a package of tissues. Her hands shook.

She removed her makeup as best she could with water and a couple of tissues.

Never in her wildest imaginings had she envisioned Zach, or any man, seeing her like this. Her appearance was the one thing she could always keep under her control.

When her tissues were black with mascara and beige from the heavy foundation she used to cover her freckles, she used one more tissue to remove whatever traces were left.

Done, she turned to Zach, slowly because this really wasn't what she wanted or what she had ever intended to happen. She held her breath and met his eyes.

He stared for a protracted moment, dark eyes thoughtful, and then broke into a broad grin that took her breath away.

"Why are you laughing at me?" She sounded like such a querulous child.

"I'm not laughing. I'm smiling. Big difference."

"Why are you smiling?"

"Because it's good to see you. It's great to see *you* again. I haven't seen this version of you in years."

"Don't tell me." Feeling downright militant, she crossed her arms. "You're one of those people who thinks makeup is bad."

He frowned. "No, I don't. I think people have a right to be whoever they want to be. Your body is your own to do with whatever you want."

"So why tell me it's good to see *me* again as though who I choose to be now isn't valid?"

He held up his hands, palms out. "I didn't mean that. I just—you're a beautiful woman, Nadine, and I find you attractive. I always have. But back in high school when I had a crush on you, your curls…your freckles…"

I find you attractive. That felt good. So good—whoa, wait. He'd had a crush on her? She stared, wide-eyed.

Zach realized what he'd said. "I just admitted to too much, didn't I?"

"You liked my freckles?"

"Oh, yeah, I sure did."

Really?

"I liked your face. A lot. Your smile."

"I don't want this wide mouth." *You look just like your mother.*

"Your smiles come all the way up from your heart. They put the sun to shame, Nadine."

Zach might sound poetic, but she didn't believe him.

Don't laugh. It's unattractive. Stop smiling with that ridiculously wide mouth. You look like a clown.

She couldn't share that with Zach, but how could two accounts of her looks be so completely different? So contradictory?

"I don't want these freckles," she said, sidestepping the confusing issue of her big mouth.

"I like them," Zach said. "I used to—"

He stopped abruptly and she regretted that. He used to…what?

"I thought you'd gotten rid of them somehow. How come they don't show anymore?"

"It's easy with the right foundation, Zach."

"So long as it's not permanent."

"It almost was. I had laser surgery booked, but then I—" She'd almost revealed everything with one little slip of her tongue. God, that was close. She'd chickened out of permanent change at the last minute, maybe her last small rebellion against Aunt Denise.

"Then you—?" Zach circled one hand as though prompting her to continue. "What?"

"Nothing."

"Whatever," he said. "As long as you don't lose them permanently, I'm happy."

She cocked her head. "But it has nothing to do with you. This is my face. I get to do whatever I want with it."

"I know. You're beautiful with or without makeup. Look, Nadine, I'm not making a judgment. It's just great to see you the way I used to—"

Again, he stopped short. Used to *what*?

"This isn't artifice," she clarified, in case he thought it was. "It isn't me needing to be fake. It's just the way I like to look. I like makeup."

"Okay. Really. I understand." He sat down on one of

the beds. She sat on the one opposite. "How about your hair? Why do you straighten it?" He gestured toward her. "Same thing. It's your choice, but what's wrong with all of those wild curls? They're amazing."

"Curls?" She ran to the mirror again. She'd been so focused on her ruined mascara that she'd failed to notice the rain had turned her shoulder-length hair to its normal mess of curls.

She brushed back her drying hair with disdainful hands.

"This isn't what I want. I want tame hair."

"What's wrong with being a little wild?" he asked. Zach looked truly puzzled while all Nadine could hear was the loop of her aunt's voice.

Fix your hair. Comb out those stupid curls.

It took her a good twenty minutes every morning to not only tame them, but to straighten them out of existence.

"So you don't like me covering my freckles *and* you don't like me straightening my curls?" She sounded like she was spoiling for a fight, and maybe she was. It was better than feeling hurt.

"Stop right there. I'm telling you I find you attractive either way, but long red hair in messy curls? It was definitely a turn-on in high school. I wasn't the only guy who wanted to touch it."

She didn't respond, didn't know how to handle these compliments, when it brought back memories of every negative comment aimed at her in those vulnerable teenage years.

But was Zach really body-shaming her or did he truly like her both ways?

"Come. Sit." His voice had gone quiet. He directed her to the spot beside him on the bed.

"Why?"

"Because somehow you're not getting what I'm really saying and we need to get past that."

She sat down.

"You were an amazing teenager, Nadine. You had these great quirky looks that you got rid of when you went away."

Enough was enough. "And now I don't look natural and so I'm bad. This is body-shaming."

"Stop it." He sounded frustrated. "Will you listen to me? I like you. I find you attractive. When you straighten your hair, it looks like red glass. It's beautiful. I also used to like your curls and your freckles. There's no problem with how you look, Nadine. Then or now."

Her problems were all internal. She picked at a thread hanging from the blanket on the bed. "It still *feels* like body-shaming."

Sap popped in a log in the fire, startling her.

"Nadine?"

"Yes?"

"When you went to New York to journalism school?"

"Uh-huh."

"And they told you to change your appearance to fit into the job?"

Seeing where he was going, she refused to answer.

"What did you call that?"

She didn't respond.

He forged on despite her refusal to participate in the discussion. "Wasn't that body-shaming?"

She stayed stony and cold.

"Your freckles were beautiful and your curly hair was…was…"

She surged to her feet. All that was in her heart, her

regrets, those very concerns, the pressure she'd felt from her professors, rang through her. Beat her up.

Yes, she'd lost little bits of herself, but look what she had gained in exchange. An exciting career. The respect of her colleagues. The adoration of her fans.

"It's none of your business," she said, angry and fierce. "You have no right to criticize. Let it go."

She tried to step away from Zach, but before she knew what he was about, he grasped her wrist and tugged, bringing her down onto his lap. He put a firm arm around her shoulders.

She wanted to resist, but she'd missed this. She'd missed being with a man. She wanted…

His face inches from hers, hazel eyes intense, he whispered, "I *like* your slimmer body. I *liked* your curvier body." His hand caressed her thigh. Holy Hannah, her traitorous body reacted. Boy, did it react, warmth forging a trail behind his fingertips. For a big man with a forceful personality, he could be gentle.

"I *liked* your freckles. I *like* when you don't have freckles." He stroked her nose with one finger, from one cheek to the other. A tingle followed its callused journey.

"And I *love* your hair. And I *loved* your hair when it was always like this. Untamed. I always wanted to do this." He delved his fingers into the thickness of it, wild and uncontrolled because of the rain. "Don't you get it, Nadine? I like *you*."

She couldn't breathe. How tall was this mountain? Was it high altitude or something? What had happened to all of the oxygen in the air?

"And this." He kissed her, his mouth meeting hers before she could turn away, hard and soft, cool and hot. Or maybe she didn't want to turn away, not when he tasted like fresh air and summer rain. He disturbed her fragile, tenuous equilibrium.

She sank into him, curled into his arms, delved into his mouth with her tongue and savored him in this private little cocoon forgotten by time and outside forces. Hidden from the world. Safe. Intact.

Herself.

She had wanted. For a long time, she had wanted this. How had she not realized that she'd wanted *him*?

He bent her over his arm until she lay on the bed and he was on top of her, his weight forceful and hefty. He pulled her closer to him, his muscled arms contracting underneath her. He parted her legs with his thigh—oh, his long, heavy thigh—and she tingled everywhere, from her throbbing private places to the tips of her fingers.

A tendril of reason, the finest filigree of common sense, tickled her judgment and she pulled her lips away from his beautiful, ravenous mouth.

No, ravenous wasn't right. He hadn't demanded. He hadn't lost control. He had savored and adored her lips.

She traced his finely sculpted mouth with her finger, met his passion-hazed gaze and said, "No."

He eased away from her by increments, then sat on the edge of the bed and leaned forward, elbows on his knees.

"Nadine." His voice came out a husky croak. He peered at her over his shoulder. "What's holding you back?"

She curled her hands under her head and stared at the ceiling. It would take only a word or two to get started, to tell him everything. To finally ask someone else to help her carry her burden. But why?

Zach didn't deserve all of her neurotic thoughts. He didn't need the truth of her past.

She didn't need the encumbrance of her past. Why foist it onto someone else?

Zach sighed. "I'm sorry, Nadine. I shouldn't have asked."

She shrugged, trying to minimize what had just happened. She couldn't give it a lot of weight. It had to mean nothing because she planned to betray the man. She didn't need an attachment to Zach to make it harder still.

She pulled herself together. The difference between Zach and her aunt was that Zach meant no harm. But he'd reminded Nadine of her own lack of confidence.

"We'll be stuck here tonight," Zach murmured. Heavy rain beat on the roof.

"Are you sure?" Her voice sounded calm, surprising her. She was doing a better job of seeming normal than she felt.

"I've ranched here all my life," Zach said. He, too, sounded normal, even after that unprecedented passion. Unprecedented for her, at any rate. Maybe he brought a lot of women here?

No, probably not. He was devoted to his boys. She couldn't see Zach sneaking off to bring women here.

"I know the weather patterns," he said. "I don't think this will end soon."

"Have you been stranded often?"

He stood and added another log to the fire. "It doesn't take much for a storm to become bad enough to make travel, especially on horseback, uncomfortable."

Zach stood abruptly. "We'd better start dinner."

A thought struck. Maybe her background as a journalist made her too suspicious.

"Did you plan this?"

For a moment, he looked lost. Uncomprehending.

"I mean," she clarified. "Did you think we would get stuck here?"

"No. I don't control the weather."

Maybe not, but… "You must have known it was going to rain."

"Sure, but not a torrential downpour. It isn't the rain that's a concern as much as the lightning."

It had been bad and she was happy to be warm and dry while rain continued to pound the windows. She liked the thought of the cabin's coziness more than the discomfort of spending the night with Zach without his boys as a buffer.

They made sandwiches together.

Heat rolled off Zach's powerful body. She liked it. She really wished she was closer to being a normal woman and could burrow against his chest.

Normal, Nadine? Really? What on earth is normal?

Maybe that was a poor choice of word. She wished she could be natural with men. There. That described things accurately.

She would love to be relaxed and not have to analyze every single word and every little action to death. She wished she were the kind of woman who could give in to temptation and a glorious one-night stand.

She shivered a little.

Zach noticed. From the armoire, he pulled out another thick plaid shirt and handed it to her. "You'll feel the dampness for a while until your hair dries and the fire warms up the cabin."

She slipped her arms through the huge sleeves, doubling up on flannel. "Thank you," she breathed, already enjoying the weight of the fabric. She rolled the sleeves to her wrists.

Their early dinner of simple sandwiches hit the spot

after getting drenched. They sat cross-legged on the carpet in front of the hearth, Zach eating like it was serious business. Nadine supposed it was for anyone who
worked a ranch.

Canned fruit cocktail made up dessert. It wasn't New
York, but it filled Nadine's stomach in this cabin, after
being caught in the rainstorm, in a deeply satisfying way.
They washed the dishes together and put them away.

Zach hung up the damp dishtowel on a nail, threw
out the dishwater and rinsed the bucket with fresh water.

When he turned back from the door, he said, "You
used to be head of the chess club in high school."

"You have a good memory."

"I used to like playing chess."

"Why didn't you join the club?"

"I couldn't join in after-school activities when there
was always work to be done on the ranch."

"Oh. Of course." They'd lived different lives.

"Do you still play?" he asked.

"I haven't in years."

Zach slid open a drawer in the bottom of the armoire
and there, stacked neatly, were all kinds of board games
and decks of cards. "If you get stuck up here, there's
nothing to do but talk or play board games."

"Let's play chess." It had been far too long. Her fingers itched to get at the men.

The interior of the cabin grew dim early in the evening.

They played for hours, evenly matched. He won, she
won, he won, she won and so it went. It turned out they
were both thoughtful people who liked the *doing* of the
game, the thinking, more than the actual winning.

As dusk settled around them, Zach put the game away,
stretched and scratched his stomach. "I'm hungry again."

From the pantry, he took out a large plastic bin. He rummaged inside it for a moment before pulling out a bag of chips. He grinned. "Ranch hands get the munchies."

"I'm surprised they left any."

"Whoever gets stuck out here is responsible for re-stocking within the next few days. I'll ride out tomorrow or the next day to replace what we've used. Maybe pick up a few extras. It's vital that we take care of this cabin," he explained. "I've had to wait out early snow-storms here. Food and fuel are essential, especially if you're stuck for longer than one night. That can be a possibility with a snowstorm."

"I guess. What kind of chips are they?"

"Oh, oh. Rafe must have stocked the place last."

"Why?"

"Honey mustard. You okay with that? It's a weird flavor."

"Are you kidding? It's my favorite. I need to meet this Rafe guy."

Zach's face shuttered faster and tighter than a crab's behind. "No. You don't."

Ohhhh. Myyy. Zach Brandt was jealous. When had that ever happened to her before? And didn't it feel incredible? Nadine smiled. She might not want a relationship with the man, but there was no denying how good it felt that he found her attractive, curly hair, freckles and all.

She held out her hand. "Chips, please."

They munched in companionable silence, Zach eating chips by the handful, while Nadine ate them one at a time.

As bedtime neared, her tension mounted. *Don't dream. Not tonight.* She couldn't stand to show vulnerability in front of Zach. Not again.

Finally, Nadine crawled between the sheets.

"Goodnight," she whispered.

"Night," he said, sounding not the least bit self-conscious.

The camaraderie of the evening evaporated in the awkwardness of sharing a dark room with a man. The fun and ease of the games of chess gave way to worry.

Zach must not have felt the same way. In minutes, soft snores drifted from the bed against the wall.

Nadine, on the other hand, lay awake for hours, tossing first one way and then the other, again and again.

Sleep must have overtaken her at some point because she awoke to a voice.

"Nadine, wake up." Then more firmly with a shake of her shoulder, "Nadine! Wake up."

She clawed her way up out of the familiar watery darkness, out of the suffocation of black concrete in her lungs, out of terror.

"Wha—?" She swallowed to moisten her dry tongue. "What?"

"You were screaming." Zach hovered above her.

She groaned. *No.* Exactly what she had wanted to avoid. She closed her eyes. "I'm so sorry."

"Don't be. It didn't bother me. I was worried about you going through your nightmare again." He sat on the side of the bed, as he had on the night with the boys in the room.

Her traitorous body said, *Touch me.*

"I woke you so you wouldn't keep having your dream."

She raised a shaking hand to her lips.

"Are you cold?" he asked.

"Yes." Her voice came out as an odd puff of air.

"I'll build the fire. Close your eyes. Go back to sleep. We've got about another hour and a half of darkness."

Zach did as he promised, building a fire that wouldn't roast her but would take the chill out of the air.

She heard his bed rustle after he got into it. He must not have been too affected by the disturbance, judging by the snoring already starting.

She had hoped that her confessions would have ended the dreams, but no. Thank God humiliation wasn't fatal. Apparently, it also didn't keep her awake.

She awoke in daylight, the smell of coffee filling the room. When she stirred, Zach said, "I'll make you tea."

"Thanks. I'll be out in a minute." She used the composting toilet in the miniscule bathroom and washed up as best she could, taking a minute to stare at herself.

Maybe she didn't look so bad.

I like you, Zach had said, in more ways than one.

Zach liked her, any way she chose to look. She sighed. If only she could feel that way about herself.

She stepped into the main room and emptied her used water out the door. The morning air was fresh, but cool. She closed the door and watched him work quietly at the counter. No other person she'd met had more integrity than Zach. If he said he liked her, it was true. If he said he liked her hair curly or straight, then he did.

Nadine's problem, she realized, was that she didn't know what to do with that information, or if she *should* do anything with it.

Zach was dressed in yesterday's clothes, dry now. He handed her a mug of hot tea and a plate of toast.

"Thank you." She couldn't meet his eye.

"Nadine." At his serious tone, she looked up. "It was only a dream."

"It was a scream in the middle of the night," she said.

"Yep. Is that so bad? We were out here in the middle of nowhere. No one heard it but us. Relax."

When she didn't respond and looked down at her plate, he bent his knees to meet her eyes. "Okay?" he asked.

Her shoulders eased. "Okay."

After breakfast, he found plastic-wrapped tooth-brushes and small travel boxes of toothpaste.

"That's a magical armoire," she said.

"Yeah. There's a bit of everything here, for any eventuality."

He brushed his teeth, not the least bit self-conscious about doing it in front of her. She used the privacy of the bathroom.

"I'll get the horses ready. See you outside."

She dressed in her own clothes, which were stiff from air-drying. The seams of her jeans were only slightly damp and not uncomfortable. On a hook by the door hung one lone straw cowboy hat. She put it on. Hers had blown off in the storm yesterday. If she didn't cover up, she would be as red as a radish later.

In front of the small shed, Zach waited with both horses.

Despite his reassurances, chagrin sat hot and heavy inside of her. It would take a whole lot more than a few compliments from Zach before she got over all the damage her aunt had done.

Zach touched one finger to the bottom of her chin and lifted her face. "There's nothing to be embarrassed about, Nadine. I told you. Sometimes the boys have bad dreams, too."

"But they don't have the same reason to dream as I do." And it left her cold and troubled.

"Someday you'll have to come to terms with that," Zach said.

How? That was the big question. How?

THANK GOD THEY were away from the cabin, Zach thought. He couldn't spend much more time alone in that small space with Nadine. It had been one thing to be there with her and his boys, but something else altogether to be alone with her.

The odd times he'd awakened during the night, he'd heard every turn she made, every soft, breathy exhalation and every brush of her flannel shirt against the blankets.

Come on, Zach. You couldn't have heard that.

But he would swear on a stack of Bibles he was that sensitive where Nadine was concerned.

Then there'd been that mind-blowing kiss...and having to pull back from it. If he'd had his way, they would have made love last night.

He disliked how hard she was on herself about everything, especially about her looks. No one should have to live such a self-conscious life. *Why* was she so hard on herself?

"How are you feeling?" he asked. "Do you still want to ride around the mountain like we'd originally intended, or would you rather head back?"

"Let's do it. I want to see what you wanted to show me."

It seemed that once he'd told her to relax about her dream, she was ready to take him at his word. He appreciated her trust in him. "Let's go then."

It took only half an hour to ride over to the vantage point Zach often used to watch Tommy.

"What am I supposed to be seeing?" Nadine asked.

"Give it a minute." He waited and then pointed. "There. That."

Chapter Eight

"Is that an elk?" Nadine asked.

"Yes."

He could feel her watching him. "So he has an elk on his land? What's wrong with that?"

"Tommy's started to pluck them from the wild and fence them in."

"Why?"

"He's setting up a game farm." Zach waited, giving her room to sort it out for herself. "It's legal, but I don't like it."

It didn't take long for her to figure out the purpose of the farm. "He's capturing animals and allowing visitors to hunt and shoot them."

Zach nodded grimly "Those elk are called shooter bulls. Sometimes they aren't even hunted down. They're in shooting enclosures. Hunters, and I use the term loosely, walk up on the other side of the fence and just shoot them. They take the antlers home as a souvenir."

"I've heard of these operations cropping up throughout the west. The owners make good money."

"Yeah, the money rolls in a hell of a lot faster and easier than with ranching."

"But it's not illegal."

"No."

"Then why are we looking at it?"

"You want to know about me and how much I love the land. I love the creatures on this land, too, and that—" he pointed below "—is cruel and unnatural."

"And you want me to write about it?"

"Only if you want to. I'm just giving you a glimpse into what works for me and what doesn't. We've got this great, amazing country with precious wildlife. I'd like to see the old ranching ways preserved and this kind of thing made illegal, but that's not going to happen when there's good money involved."

"Are you trying to do anything about it?"

"No. Tommy's exercising his legal right to do with his land whatever he wants." Zach jerked a thumb over his shoulder. "I prefer to grow crops and graze cattle and sell them for their meat. Maybe I'm no better than Tommy. Maybe I should become a vegetarian, but I won't. Those animals Tommy captures aren't even killed for their meat, though. It would be easier to accept this bogus hunting if they were."

He stared at the Broome property for a long moment, wishing like hell Tommy had never done this so close to his land.

"Let's go," he said, and rode away slowly so Nadine would have no trouble keeping up.

BEFORE GOING INTO the office, Nadine showered and changed clothes in her apartment, applying her makeup meticulously. Then she sat down and transcribed the notes she'd recorded before the rain hit yesterday. She also wrote her impressions of what Zach had shown her this morning.

She didn't want any of this on her computer downstairs. She didn't know if Lee could access her computer, but she wasn't taking chances. She no longer trusted the man.

"How come I don't have an article on my desk?" Lee asked the moment she entered the newsroom.

"Lee, you know it can take me a couple of weeks to complete interviews and then write it up. I've edited your articles for the next issue. You've edited my columns. There were a lot of announcements this week, so they're long. You have a couple of articles from that freelancer you use. That's a full issue. What's the rush?"

"Never you mind." Lee bit a nail and seemed to reconsider. "The story will sell papers," he admitted. "If it's as good a secret as my mother hinted, then people will want to know about it. The sooner we get it out there, the better."

Gossip. Titillation. She hadn't studied journalism for this, but he was right. It sure did sell. And if she didn't produce something for Lee, he would fire her.

Norma hadn't disclosed a lot to Nadine, but she thought she knew what might work. Would her conscience let her do it? But she had to get the information for Lee.

"Nadine." His voice intruded on her thoughts.

"Yes?"

"I called my mother a half an hour ago when I was waiting for you to come in."

She knew what he was going to say and didn't want to hear it. *No. Don't open your mouth. Don't taint what was the most beautiful—the easiest—night I've ever spent with a man so soon after it's happened.*

But reality was intruding.

"She's lucid today. Get out there and talk to her."

"Sure."

In a repeat performance of the visit she made to

Norma the week before, Nadine got only so far with her before Norma lost patience with dredging up ancient history. Nadine left the nursing home knowing, *knowing* beyond a shadow of a doubt, how to get Norma to talk. She couldn't bring herself to do it.

Buying herself another day, she invited Rick to the diner for coffee.

In her interview with him, she came away with details about Zach's childhood. No, he and his wife weren't the source for Zach's love of art. Yes, it had all come from inside the child himself.

Despite skillful questioning, Nadine came away from the interview convinced that Rick had no secrets. Did no one in the family know about Zach's possible heritage other than the ancestors who were now dead?

She spent the afternoon working on the article in her apartment. She didn't want Lee breathing down her neck.

Afterward, she sent out ads for the renewed rodeo and fair, using up the two thousand dollars Sam had given her. Her role in the fair committee's organization was finished for now.

She'd enjoyed the whole process and being such an important part of the fair revival. She only hoped she'd done enough.

But wait? What about the writing contest?

She ran into Lee in the office.

"I've had people drawn in by the poster in the window," he said, sounding excited. "It's generating interest. Apparently, kids are out there writing stories. Good idea, Nadine. I like it."

"I'd like to help judge once the entries come in."

"Sure. No problem. Let's pull in another couple of people as well. The mayor. The sheriff. Make it a big deal."

There Lee went being nice again. Dealing with him these days was like being on a roller coaster ride.

That night she fell into bed with her mind in turmoil and was awakened several times by different dreams, of Zach kissing her and of Zach hating her. Heaven and hell.

In the morning, she awoke tired and grumpy. She showered, dressed, styled her hair and applied her makeup, even though it was Saturday.

Before she'd even had time to make coffee, the doorbell rang. Who on earth? Thank goodness she was dressed. She trudged downstairs to answer the door.

ZACH STOOD AT Nadine's apartment door with a couple of takeout coffees from the diner and two of Vy's custard-filled donuts.

He'd never been here before. He knew he was invading her space, but he felt they'd left things…unresolved yesterday. After the night in the cabin, he wanted more than ever to find out what went on inside of Nadine. Some of the things she'd said had disturbed him.

Nadine answered the door attired and made up to perfection. "What are you doing here?" She didn't sound rude, only surprised.

Zach had thought she might still be in her pajamas or a bathrobe or something, but she was back to her current version of herself. He missed those curls. They could tempt a sane man into all kinds of naughty dreams. Erotic dreams. Amazing, kick-ass dreams.

And her freckles. Auburn, a shade darker than her hair, but less bright, larger on her nose and tinier across her cheeks. One, he'd noticed, straddled her upper lip. That pretty little dot had tempted him to kiss her every time he'd looked at her at the cabin.

But it was all gone today, covered by foundation. Too bad.

Or maybe not. She was who she was. The more he learned about her, the more she fascinated him.

"Zach? What are you doing here?" she repeated.

"We need to talk."

The suggestion of a frown appeared on her forehead. "Okay. Come on up."

Upstairs, he found her apartment as confined and neat and tidy as she was. Not a magazine, not a dirty coffee mug, not a single sock lay around. It looked better than a house done up for a magazine shoot.

What must she have thought of the chaos of his house? And his boys?

"What do you want to talk about?" she asked.

You. Your past. "A couple of things you said at the cabin."

She drew inside of herself. He wasn't sure how he could tell, but he sensed a deeper stillness in her.

"What things?" She stepped into the kitchen, putting the counter that separated it from the living room between herself and Zach.

Zach pulled out a stool on the living room side and sat down. "About why you grew up thinking there was something wrong with your appearance."

She stared at him coldly.

"I have no intention of leaving until I get the truth," he said. "When you talked about James, you said, and I quote, 'I thought *I'd* been mistreated.' You meant when you were a teenager. Talk to me."

"You're bullying me."

"Am I? That's not my intention."

"What is?"

"I think you need to talk about whatever happened back then."

"*You* think? That's arrogant, Zach. Do you honestly believe you know what's best for me?"

"I know that I care for you and I think repression isn't good for anyone." He didn't want to see her hurting. He didn't want to think she harbored a bunch of hurt inside of her.

She leaned both hands on the counter, elbows locked. "You think I'm repressed."

"I think you don't like yourself very much."

She opened her mouth but he cut her off. "Considering what a truly fine person you are, I had to ask myself, why wouldn't Nadine love herself as much as her friends love her?"

She closed her mouth, maybe because he'd called her a fine person. He meant it. She was good to her core. She'd made a big mistake in the city, but she could come to terms with that in time. Zach had no doubt about that.

But there was even deeper stuff going on inside of Nadine. He wanted it out in the open so she could heal, because if she could accept herself, maybe she'd accept him into her life.

Yes, she was right. It was probably arrogance on his part, but what were friends good for if they didn't help each other?

He pushed one of the paper cups of coffee toward her while he opened the other one.

"I didn't know how you take it, but figured you'd have sugar and cream here if you needed them."

She opened her cup and sipped it black. Okay, now he knew how she liked her coffee.

He opened the box of donuts and slid them toward her.

"I don't eat those."

"No problem. I'll eat them both." He took a huge bite of one. No one did custard-filled donuts like Vy did. He chewed, swallowed and sipped coffee.

"I can do this all day, you know," he said while she watched him. "Eat donuts and drink coffee and wait for you to open up. I'm not going anywhere until we have this conversation."

"You are *so* arrogant."

Zach laughed without taking offense. "Probably true."

She huffed. "Ooooh, you make it hard to stay mad at you."

"I do? Tell me how so I can do it again in the future."

She shook her head. She laughed. She gave in. "Fine. You are so stubborn."

"Yeah, I've heard that before. So talk."

"If I'm going to lay my soul bare, let's at least get comfortable." She rounded the counter and curled up in an armchair in the living room. Zach took the sofa across from her.

She stared at him with defiance, as though already deciding he wouldn't believe her. "My aunt Denise wasn't the nicest woman around."

That surprised Zach. Sure, he'd had his suspicions lately, but hearing it stated baldly shocked him. Everyone in Rodeo had liked her. "Denise sure put on a good show around town, then."

She burst out of her seat. "I *knew* you wouldn't believe me." When she tried to get around his long legs, he snagged her wrist and pulled her down onto the sofa beside him.

"I do believe you. It's just a shock. You know what she was like with everyone else. Obviously, a lot nicer than with you."

She swiped her fingers across her damp cheeks. She

was crying. With that one admission, a faucet had been turned on. Her hands, he noticed, shook.

Zach hunkered down to see into her eyes. "A *hell* of a lot nicer?" he asked, seeking clarity.

She nodded. "*Hell* is a good word for what I lived through with her."

"Tell me about it." Fingers gentle around her arm, he pleaded, "Please talk. I want you to be happy."

"Why?" The anguish on her face tore at him.

"Because I care about you. Because I don't like to see you hurting." He set his cup on the coffee table. "Because I think you've held something bad or troubling inside for a lot of years and it's time to let it out."

"Why do you think I'm holding anything in?"

He took one of her hands in his and played with her fingers. She had eloquent hands. Even while the face she showed to the world every day was cool, her hands told a different story, active and expressive. Bits of her inner character leaked through in her gestures.

"Because you used to laugh more. When you were really young, when you first came to town, you had a bold, happy laugh. It started to disappear when we entered high school. It came less and less frequently as the grades passed. Now it's gone completely. I want to hear it again."

Her full lips had curled in on themselves.

"Don't hold back," he urged gently. "It's time to talk."

She sighed. "You asked for it."

She curled into the corner between the back of the sofa and the arm, twisting her legs up under her. She crossed her arms as though to hold herself together.

"I need to go back to the beginning. Aunt Denise was my mother's sister. My mother died when I was eleven. That's when I came here to live with my aunt."

"I remember."

She startled. "You do?"

"Sure. You were new to town. I was curious. You were young and gangly, but you had that great wide smile and all of that curly red hair."

"Oh, my hair. Aunt Denise despaired of it. The curls would get so tangled. She was rough with it."

"Why did you have to come here? Couldn't your father take care of you?"

She studied her knees. "I never knew my biological father. The man who died in the car with my mom was my stepfather. I called him Dad, though. I loved him."

He squeezed her hand. "I'm sorry. If you don't mind my asking, what happened with your biological father?"

"It was a rare one-night stand for my mother." Her cheeks turned red, glowing even through her foundation. "She got caught. She was pregnant with no idea how to find him."

"How did that affect you growing up?"

"Mom and I had a good life together. We had fun until she found my stepfather and got married. Then we had an even better life. He was a good man. I didn't know I should be ashamed about my past until I came here to live with Denise."

"Denise *made* you feel embarrassed about it?"

"Did she ever! She said I should never tell anyone. She was ashamed of my mother."

Zach picked up a strand of hair that had fallen forward and tucked it behind her ear. She shivered. "Do you look like your mother or your father?"

"Very much like my mother. She and Denise looked totally different. My mother took after their mother and Denise after their father."

Zach began to guess some of what had been going

on, the dynamic that might have occurred within that family. If Nadine resembled her mother, then she had been a beautiful woman. Denise was short and plump, but even if she'd had more conventional good looks, he imagined Nadine's mother's beauty would have over-shadowed her own.

Acting on a hunch, he asked, "So Denise gave you a hard time about your appearance?"

"Yes," Nadine whispered. "All of the time. Apparently, not only had my mother taught me how to do everything wrong, but I was also goofy-looking. Denise said boys would never like me."

"They did."

"What?"

"Boys. They liked you."

"How do you know?"

"Because I did." He smiled. "I was a boy."

She smiled tentatively in return, but he wanted to see that pretty, wide mouth fully involved in a laugh.

"Keep going," he said. "What did she complain about?"

"Everything. As far as the way I did things, she criticized it all, day after day after day. My mother had been fun-loving and affectionate. Denise was neither. The criticism wore me down."

She twined her fingers with his. As far into her memories as she was, Zach didn't think she even noticed that he held her hand.

"At first, I thought I could make her happy by changing the way I did things, but that never happened. I changed everything I'd ever been taught by my mother and it still wasn't enough for Denise. You know, I really think that putting me down was a sport for her."

"It never ended."

"It never ended," Nadine confirmed with a curse, her anger finally unleashed. Zach was glad to see it. "My mouth was too wide. My lips were too big. My *body* was too big. No, wait. That came later, after I hit puberty. Then she told me I was fat and watched every single piece of food I put into my mouth."

Zach remembered how she'd filled out. Her curves were beautiful and she should have never been put to shame about her body. Denise must have been envious.

"My hair was too red and too curly. She called me carrot-top."

He would have never guessed Denise had that much viciousness inside of her. She'd walked around town as though butter wouldn't melt in her mouth.

What Denise had dished out was abuse, pure and simple.

Zach had a suspicion. "When you went away to college and they told you your looks were too unconventional for television, what did you think?"

Her green eyes widened. "That Aunt Denise had been right all along, of course."

"That's what I thought."

Nadine fiddled with the fringe of a cushion in her lap. "You think they were wrong."

"I do. You're ambitious and smart. Maybe that would have been enough."

"I didn't think so. The world of journalism, especially on TV where reporters are visible, is wildly competitive. You take whatever edge you can get and change whatever will hold you back."

"I'll bow to your superior authority in that area."

She shot him a sidelong glance. "Are you being sarcastic?"

"No. You know that industry, and I don't. I would

think that a woman who's as smart as you could make it despite any defects you *perceive* in your looks."

"Those defects—"

He cut her off. "Don't exist in my book. You were beautiful when you left here. There wasn't a thing wrong with you."

"Have you looked at TV anchors lately? Male or female?"

"I don't really notice. I go to the news shows to find out what's happening in the world."

"I'm going to hazard a guess that you don't notice them because they don't stand out in any strange ways. The women are beautiful, but not outrageously so. They also aren't quirky. Had I done nothing to improve—"

"Change."

"—*improve* my appearance, they would never have hired me."

Zach bit his tongue, trying his hardest to not insist that in an ideal world, looks wouldn't matter. Intelligence and the ability to do a great job would. When had the world ever been ideal?

The Nadine who had left Rodeo a decade ago to conquer the field of journalism would have put her heart into her career. But maybe that wouldn't have mattered in corporate TV land. Nadine knew that world. Zach didn't. But what a damned shame.

He frowned. "But you're back home now. Why can't you drop the mask and change back to who you were?"

"It's not a mask!"

Again, Zach bit his tongue. He hadn't meant to say it like that. They'd been over this last night, after all, and he should respect her choices. But he remembered Nadine's coltish exuberance when she'd come to town as a young girl. He wanted it back, for her sake. Nadine deserved to be happy.

She was right about one thing, though. Her appearance was her business and hers alone, despite the negativity behind her choices. He had no right to tell her what she should be doing with any of it.

Still she fiddled with the pillow fringe. Her face appeared calm, but yet again her fingers belied that impression. They moved restlessly, dancing in their constant, unconscious manifestation of Nadine's inner turmoil. Her true nature seeking release?

At that moment, he wanted to hold her. To pick her up and curl her body against his, curve his body around hers in return to protect her from anyone who had ever told her she wasn't good enough.

Instead, he said, "You. You are perfectly, supremely you. You are perfect. I don't care what anyone else thinks. Curly or straight hair, made up or not, slim or full-figured…" In this precious time and place, he would like to make love with her.

Would she let him?

Only one way to find out.

She stared at him as though he'd handed her the moon. Her lower lip trembled.

He reached for her, but she moved farther into the corner of the sofa. Lord, was there a metaphor in there somewhere? Was she moving farther into the corner of her life that Denise and TV network executives had so narrowly prescribed for her?

"Can I ask you a question?"

A funny smile twisted her mouth. "You've already asked a lot of them. Why stop now?"

Zach's lips quirked up. "I understand that journalism

is important to you. Why was it important for you to be on television?"

"I hate to be too honest. You'll probably think less of me."

"Hey, this is me. Zach. I won't judge." His curiosity shot through the roof. What could Nadine have to say that would be so bad?

"I guess I wanted to be visible. I wanted to prove Aunt Denise wrong when she told me I was ugly and awkward and unlovable."

"She *was* wrong. You were never any of those things. Denise was the only one who ever thought that. I'll bet if you asked anyone in town, they would all tell you it's hogwash."

She shrugged.

He hadn't convinced her. She still had something to prove. "Do your friends know about Denise and her criticisms?" he asked.

"A bit, yes. I told them this week."

"Can you do something for me?" he asked.

"What's that?"

"Can you talk to them some more? You still don't believe how much respect you deserve. Maybe Honey or Vy will stand a better chance of convincing you than I can."

She stared toward the picture window at the front of the apartment. "I don't know, Zach."

"Think about it. Okay?"

"Okay."

"Promise."

"Yes, I promise."

He got to his feet. She followed suit. He denied himself what he really wanted to do, which was to wrap her in his arms and kiss the daylights out of her. Her vulnerability held him off.

Instead, he leaned forward slowly, giving her time to pull back if she wanted to. He set his lips on hers and kissed her with a restraint he didn't want to exercise, but which she needed.

I like you, his lips said. *I believe in you.*

He left it at that.

It was as much as she would take at the moment.

NADINE SAT AT the diner in a booth across from Honey Armstrong. She had promised Zach she would tell her friends. She'd chosen Honey first. Honey had an amazing head on her shoulders, full of all kinds of common sense.

Zach's visit had disturbed Nadine on so many levels. She hadn't wanted to share so much, but the unburdening had been beyond anything she might have imagined. She felt lighter. She felt younger.

She felt robbed.

Zach may have given her a gift with his listening ear, but he'd also given her another burden. Nadine could no longer keep all of her resentment toward Aunt Denise tamped down and buried.

She didn't know what to do with the anger.

Zach's reaction had been unadulterated support. Maybe she should have opened up sooner. She might have had relief from the dishonesty of pretending to like and love her aunt. Maybe she should have told the townspeople how Denise really was.

On the other hand, airing dirty family linen was exhausting.

You. You are perfectly, supremely you.

Oh, Zach.

If a heart could tumble into love, hers had done so when Zach had given her that gift.

So now she knew she was in love. In love! With Zach.

Yet another burden. While Lee's need for dirt hung over her head, she could never explore her feelings.

Zach had given Nadine a precious gift and yet she sank into despair.

Vy came over to take their orders. "You all ready for the wedding tomorrow?"

Wedding?

Oh, no. In all of the turmoil of the past week, and amid Lee's awful demands and the new realization of her devastating feelings for Zach, Nadine had forgotten about Honey's wedding.

"I can't wait," Honey said. "It's going to be a great party. Chet's taking care of the bar tonight. I've got extra waiters coming in to work because it's Saturday night. I have the night off so I can rest up for my big day."

Nadine smiled, happy for Honey and Cole.

"I'm looking forward to it," she said, even if her heart was not completely in it. She would have to adjust her attitude by tomorrow.

Over coffee and salad, she told Honey everything she had shared with Zach that morning. The full story. Honey's beautiful, generous response warmed Nadine through and through.

"I wish I had known back then. I would have come to your rescue. I would have given Denise a piece of my mind."

Nadine smiled. "You would have, wouldn't you? Even as a teenager."

"You bet." Honey raised her cup for a refill. One of Vy's waitresses brought the pot over. Honey reached across the table and took Nadine's hands in her own. "You know we're all here for you."

Nadine nodded.

"Then share this with the other women, too. You

could have had years of support instead of carrying your pain alone."

"It was too painful to say out loud."

"I can imagine, but you've taken that step now and you know everyone else would understand."

"Understand what?" Vy had walked up with their bill. She tossed it onto the table between them.

Honey picked it up. "My treat."

Nadine didn't know if she could tell the whole thing one more time today.

Vy slid into the booth beside Honey, nudging her over with her hip, and stared at Nadine. "Why is the atmosphere at this table so heavy?"

"Don't you have work to do?" Nadine asked. God, Vy was so curious. "Customers to serve?"

"Break time. Spill."

Nadine stared, gutted and tired. She honestly didn't mind sharing with Vy, especially not after Honey's acceptance, but she didn't have any energy left.

"Do you want me to tell her?" Honey asked.

"Yes," Nadine replied, voice thin, nerves stretched to the limit. She'd worked hard to suppress her emotions since returning home, but spending time with Zach had brought it all to the surface.

Honey repeated Nadine's story.

"We love you exactly as you are, Nadine," Vy said. "Denise was wrong. About everything."

Nadine nearly wept right there in the diner. She had amazing friends.

Back in her apartment, she lay down fully dressed on top of her bed. Confessing one's past was exhausting.

She awoke to her home phone ringing. Scrambling out of bed, she lurched down the hallway and picked up the receiver.

"Hel—?" She cleared her throat and tried again. "Hello?"

"Can you come over today?"

The young voice on the other end of the phone was either Aiden or Ryan. "I wrote another story. I want you to read it."

Aiden. Phoning her. Oh, so sweet. Taking initiative. Taking care of his own business.

"Are you sure it's okay with your father for me to come out to the ranch today?"

"Yeah. You want to talk to him?" He sounded resigned, as though he was tired of adults always making decisions for him.

Poor kid. Nadine smiled. He had a decade more of it before he was free and on his own.

"Nadine?" Zach said.

"Hi. Aiden wants me to come out to the ranch to read his next story. Did you know about this? I wondered if he had your permission."

"He does. Come for supper."

"Okay. What can I bring?"

"Just yourself."

She had no idea what time it was, but said yes again, hung up and called Vy.

"Do you have any pies or desserts left? I'm going to Zach's for dinner. I'd like to take something."

"I have a coconut cream pie."

"It's mine. See you in half an hour."

"I'll be closed by then. How about if I bring it over?"

"I have to shower before I go."

"Fine. I have your key. I'll put it in the fridge. Pay me tomorrow."

Nadine showered, changed her clothes and reapplied her makeup. She walked to the kitchen and checked her fridge. Sure enough, on the top shelf sat a fluffy home-made coconut cream pie.

With the care she might bestow on a newborn, she carried it out to the passenger seat of her car and drove to the ranch.

Ryan and Aiden met her at her car door, with Aiden practically shoving his story into her hands.

His enthusiasm delighted her and she laughed. "Wait until I get out of the car."

He gave her some space then tried to hand it to her again.

"Let's go sit inside," she said. "It's hot out here."

Ryan ran in circles around her, while Aiden walked more quietly beside her.

Nadine smiled at Zach and said, "There's a pie on the front seat. Can you get it?"

He looked particularly fine tonight in clean jeans and a white T-shirt that molded to his strong body. She hardened herself against the attraction she felt. She was here for Aiden, not to fuel her newfound feelings for Zach.

Aiden ran toward the living room. "Sit beside me, okay?"

Ryan took off after him, yelling, "Sit beside *me*."

Zach followed her inside and said, "Believe it or not, those kids get enough attention. They like you."

"I like them." Nadine followed them to the sofa.

"Coffee?" Zach asked.

"Decaf?"

"Can do," he said and went off to make it.

In the cool living room with a cross breeze from the windows, she sat between the two children. Only a week ago, they had made her uncomfortable. Since then, she had discovered that all she had to do was talk to them.

Or more importantly, simply listen. They liked when she gave them her undivided attention.

She liked when they crowded her and wanted to hold her hands and sit with her and make her tea and too-sweet cookies.

"Ryan, have you heard this story yet?" she asked.

He shook his head. "My brother writes good stories."

"He sure does," Nadine agreed. "I'll read it out loud."

She did and found it much like the first, with an injured animal being rescued by a brave little boy. Clearly, Aiden cast himself in the role of protagonist in his stories.

"I like it a lot, Aiden." She went on to tell him everything she liked about it, while Zach sat in an armchair and sipped coffee. His father puttered about in the kitchen with pots and pans. Nadine heard the clink and clatter of plates and cutlery as the table was being set.

Everything inside of her warmed and melted. She liked it here. She liked Zach and his father and, heaven help her, she'd fallen in love with Aiden and Ryan.

Dinner was soup, excellent homemade minestrone, and rolls and a side salad. Uncomplicated and casual. After dinner, the boys took her to the barn to see the new kittens. They played there for a while until bedtime.

Nadine found herself relaxing into a level of comfort she didn't usually experience with others, but something about unburdening herself to Zach and two of her friends had changed her in a fundamental way.

And wasn't that ironic when she would eventually change the way Zach felt about her? He would probably never talk to her again.

She ignored the clenching of her nerves. This evening was too perfect to ruin with thoughts of Lee and family secrets.

He walked her to her car. In the soft fall of twilight, in the hushed silence of the transitioning moment from day to night, he said, "Thank you."

"For what?"

"For accommodating my boys. For not ignoring them or making them feel bad about themselves just because they want a little attention."

"I don't mind at all. They're good children."

"Even with their sibling rivalry? Even with them fighting for an equal share of your attention?"

"Even with that. I was an only child, so it's all new to me. It's fun to watch."

"You're good with them."

It was time for her to leave, but she lingered. She wasn't sure why. Maybe it was the peace and serenity of the moment. Maybe that serenity had come from the confessions Zach had coaxed out of her.

"I told Honey and Vy today."

"About Denise?"

"Yes. Everything. More than I had before."

"How did they react?"

"They were thoroughly supportive."

"They're good women."

"They are." Another topic exhausted. She should leave. She didn't.

Go, Nadine. Why hang around here? Because of that seductive peace I feel beside this solid, steady man.

Zach exuded comfort and a good character. He could probably gentle the wildest horse. Apparently, he had that effect on women, too. On her, at least.

Something swooped past her head and she shrieked, the moment shattered.

Zach laughed.

"What's so funny?" Grouchy, she ducked, afraid of more flying projectiles. "What was that?"

"Only a bat."

"A *bat*? Don't they grab on to your hair and won't let go?" She covered her head with both hands.

"That's a myth. They fly around at this time of night looking for insects, that's all."

"Maybe he should stay away from me."

"Maybe you should stay out of his flight path." Zach's tone rang with humor.

Another bat swooped nearby. "On that note, I'm going home."

She got into her car and drove away wondering what tomorrow would bring.

Honey and Cole were getting married.

Nadine would see Zach and the boys again tomorrow.

Chapter Nine

Honey and Cole's wedding was held on Sunday afternoon at the bar.

The bar was closed on Sundays, so it was the perfect time to hold a private event.

Nadine dressed with care and went over a little early to meet her friends. They were decorating the place while Chet cooked up a storm. By the time guests arrived, hot pink crepe streamers hung everywhere and flowers graced every table.

When Honey stood in front of the preacher with the very handsome sheriff, Nadine's heart melted. Their love for each other fairly glowed from them. The vows they had written rang with every hope for a long future together.

Cole's children stood between them, and their closest friends formed a circle around them—Nadine included.

When Honey and Cole turned to the gathered townsfolk as husband and wife, applause erupted. Nadine couldn't see them through a blur of tears, but knew they had enormous grins on their faces.

They all ate and drank and danced long into the evening.

Aiden and Ryan stuck by Nadine's side for most of the reception. They wore little white dress shirts and clip-on bowties. They were adorable in their blue jeans and cowboy boots. Nadine danced with them to a mix of music, old and new, that Honey had chosen.

After dusk settled, children went home with parents or caregivers and the party kicked into high gear. A country band tuned up and broke into raucous tunes perfect for line dancing.

At the bar, she brushed shoulders with Zach. "Who's babysitting tonight?"

"A girl from two ranches over. You know Jessica Alton?"

"Yes. She seems dependable."

"She is. Ryan and Aiden like her."

He took a long pull from his bottle of beer, then turned and looked at her directly. "I'm footloose and fancy-free." He leaned one arm on the bar and crossed his cowboy-booted feet, about as masculine a man as Nadine had ever met.

No wonder his wife had fallen for him so fast and hard.

He gazed at her from beneath long, dark lashes and drew one finger along her jawline. Nadine shivered... and then shivered again.

She was in trouble. Deep, deep, deep trouble.

Zach cupped her shoulder with his big palm and pulled her close. He bent forward and whispered in her ear, "I'm free for the entire night," and Nadine was lost.

All of her worries, her fears of Lee and losing her job and digging up dirt and writing awful, awful things fell away. She needed tonight.

She needed Zach.

Rational thought and conscious decision gave way to acceptance. And to capitulation. She wanted this. She wanted Zach.

His hand skimmed down her arm, leaving pebbled skin in its wake. He grasped her hand and walked to the dance floor.

Like the meek little lamb she'd refused to be on her first visit to the ranch to interview him, Nadine followed.

The band eased into a slow tune, a country waltz.

Zach, as it turned out, danced oh, so beautifully. Nadine set one hand on his hard shoulder and nestled her other in his palm, where his calluses rasped deliciously against her soft skin.

Seriously, Nadine? Calluses are not *sexy.*

Oh, but they were. They *so* were.

His embrace firm, he pulled her body flush against his. She felt every one of his rock-hard muscles, including the long thighs that directed her in the dance.

"No sense slow dancing if I can't really hold you close," he whispered, his breath feathering loose strands of hair around her face.

Lost in sensation, with dancers swirling around her and colors flying and heat building between them, Nadine fell into such peace, such sureness that a night with Zach was perfect and right.

"Let's go to my place," she said.

Zach twirled her around and pulled her to the door. "I thought you'd never ask."

"I should say goodbye to my friends." She tried to pull her hand free. He held on. She smiled.

"Nope. We gotta go now."

Nadine laughed with the pure pleasure of seeing controlled Zach unleashed, unfettered and impatient. She had done that to him.

The power was heady.

Upstairs in her apartment, they never made it to the

bed, but took each other on the plush carpet in the living room, fast and furious and hot and hard and perfect.

Nadine had controlled her passion, had subsumed her very being for too many years. With a melting of barriers, she gave all of herself to Zach and let in as much as he was willing to share.

She liked soft. She liked sensual. She liked playful affection. This searing, this burning, ravening, voracious need consumed her and she couldn't get enough of him. Aggressive and desperate for his body and his touch, she kissed him deeply, her tongue taking and giving.

Zach's big body covered hers…and she reveled in his solid weight. She welcomed him into her, wrapping herself around him to keep him safe.

Don't hurt.

Don't die.

Don't leave.

She cried out. Zach shouted.

They lay spent, Zach anchoring her to the world in a way that was foreign to her. When Nadine shivered, he rolled to his side, wrapping his arms around her. Enfolded in Zach's strength, she was safe. Secure.

She did the same for him, because she needed this man to be invincible. Since he wasn't, because he was only human, she held on to protect him.

But no, she couldn't. Could she?

She knew how imperfect and useless she was in that area. She could no more protect Zach than she could stop the Niagara from barreling over timeworn rock. She was and always would be a failure. Zach would get hurt. His children would get hurt.

But there was tonight. There were a few more hours for wonder and love. She had been missing love since

she was eleven years old. Could one night refill that de-
pleted well?

She could only try.

ZACH SENSED HER WITHDRAWAL.

After the most passionate bout of lovemaking of his
life, this vibrant, untethered version of Nadine slowly
retreated.

He tightened his arms around her, but the task of
keeping her here proved futile. She might still be in his
arms physically, but that vital Nadine had disappeared.

He hid his face in the sweet spot between her neck
and her shoulder. He kissed her there. *Please come back.*

For long, warm minutes, he lay that way because he
didn't want to see her cold mask. He didn't want to witness the transformation he felt in his arms from *here*
to *gone.*

Don't leave, Nadine, he wanted to shout but couldn't.

She had her reasons for hiding, but what were they?
He didn't think she'd held anything else back in her confessions. So why, after sublime bliss, did she deflate and
disappear?

She turned to him and kissed him, with passion, yes,
but also with desperation.

Before they made love again, Zach went to the bathroom and got rid of his condom.

When he returned to the living room, Nadine asked,
"Did you put that on in the bar?"

"The condom? No. Here." He lay down beside her.
"While we were making love. Before I entered you."

"I didn't even realize."

Zach chuckled. "I barely got it on. You were demanding." He reached for his pants and pulled out a handful
of foil packets.

Nadine stared. "You were sure of yourself."

"No. I had hopes, though." He was ready to share every bit of emotion he felt, but she forestalled him with a finger to his lips.

"Just tonight, Zach. Let's just have tonight."

He wanted to argue, but she kissed him and all thought flew from his head.

Zach gave and gave and gave because she needed. But nothing he did was enough. She needed his body and his passion, his physical lovemaking, but she was blocking anything else, even as he knew she needed more with a depth that unnerved him.

As much as he loved trying, he knew the future he'd hoped to have with her wasn't going to be the one she wanted.

Both happy and deflated, he left in the morning while she slept.

NADINE AWOKE ALONE and cried.

She'd had her one night. It had been magnificent, even while she'd been saddened knowing it wouldn't last. Even while remorse had flooded her as they'd made love.

Today. She had to rock his world today. His Broome grandfather had had a son from a previous marriage, therefore older than Rick. Tommy Broome was a few months older than Zach.

She had done her research well.

Would Tommy somehow try to lay claim to Zach's ranch? Or part of it to enlarge his game farm?

Nadine didn't know if that were possible, but it worried her.

She phoned Zach.

He answered, "Hey, lover," sounding like he was joking, but oh, that word.

Yes, last night they had been lovers, and it had been spectacular. She had bared herself to him in every way. Never before in her life, with anyone, had she shown as much of herself.

How, then, could she betray all of that beautiful loving he'd given her? He'd accepted her. Made her believe in her right to be who she wanted to be and to accept what she couldn't change about herself. He'd given her the gift of allowing her to be *her*.

Her heart ached.

Her future was on the line. She had lost her career once. Could she go through the pain of losing it again? Of losing the chance to run the paper and to stay here in town and work among her friends?

Could she bear the loneliness of moving away again if Lee fired her?

She cleared her throat and said, "Zach." She couldn't give in to his endearments, not considering what she was about to do. "Could I ask you to come somewhere with me?"

His low, sexy chuckle warmed a path down her spine. "Anywhere."

"Can you visit Norma Beeton with me?"

"Norma?" She'd surprised him. "What on earth for?"

"I'd rather you just…come."

"Okay." He sounded curious but willing. "I haven't had lunch yet."

"I'm heading to the diner. Meet me there and we can have lunch. My treat."

"Order me a BLT with mayo. Vy knows how I like it. See you in fifteen."

She walked down Main and entered the diner.

"Hey," Vy called. "Sit anywhere. Be over soon."

Nadine chose a seat at the far end of the counter. She

waved to Sheriff Cole sitting in the back booth with his two young children. A minute later, Honey Armstrong walked in and made a beeline for the table, not even seeing Nadine in her rush to see the man who had become her husband only yesterday.

Neither of them had wanted a honeymoon. They wanted their hard-won life together as a family to start immediately.

Nadine was ecstatic for both Honey and Cole, even as she acknowledged that her happiness lay in her career, not in family life.

But the twins.

Oh, God, when she betrayed Zach, she would betray them, too. How could she do that?

She should have never allowed herself to get close to them. She knew how to be a good journalist. She understood about detachment, objectivity. But those boys had worked their way into her heart and she'd begun to imagine possibilities she'd never known before. By the end of the afternoon, those dreams would be shattered.

Nope. No family of her own. Ever.

When Vy came over, Nadine placed Zach's order along with her own. She put her bag onto the stool beside her to reserve it for Zach.

True to his word, he arrived before the food did, easing his long body onto the stool with athletic grace, a body she had trouble looking away from. It seemed she was doomed to remember every inch of him, every touch, every kiss, every piece of unalloyed pleasure. Last night had been the best lovemaking of her life.

His thigh brushed hers and she shifted away from him. He wasn't a huge man and yet he took up a lot of space. She thought she felt his heat…or was it just warmth leaking from the open kitchen on the other side of the counter? She hadn't noticed it before Zach arrived.

When Vy brought Zach a coffee, she grinned. "Hey, handsome, haven't seen you in here in a while."

"Hey, yourself, good-lookin'." Zach's answering smile was full of affection and respect. "Been busy." He took Vy's hand and kissed her fingers. "When're you going to leave Sam and give me a chance?"

Nadine stared. Zach was flirting with Vy? She truly had never known this side of him before.

Vy hooted. "As if. I was single for years. Now that I'm taken, you want me? Affection is easy when you don't have to act on it."

Zach dropped her hand and grinned. "You see right through me." Laugh lines radiated from the corners of his eyes, pale against his tan. "Good party last night. I see the lovebirds are here for lunch but have eyes for no one but each other."

"True love will do that to a man and woman," Vy said, but immediately grew serious. "I heard about Tommy's new venture. The 'animal sanctuary.'" She used air quotes around the word. "It's the buzz of the town. You can't be happy about that happening almost on your doorstep."

Zach's jaw tightened to granite. "The town's divided over the issue. You know, there isn't really a win-win here. Tommy wants to make more money. He's doing it on his land, not mine, so who am I to judge?"

"I wonder how big he plans to make the enterprise?" Vy glanced between Zach and Nadine. "Are you going to get Nadine to write about it?"

"That's her business, not mine."

"She should interview Tommy. She'll find out. I swear Nadine can ferret out any secret in town."

Any secret... Vy was only joking, but why use that

word? That awful, terrible word that sent panic racing through Nadine's stomach.

And what if Tommy could take away some, or all, of Zach's land? Why hadn't she thought to research that awful possibility?

Vy got their food from the order window and carried over Zach's sandwich and a poached chicken on romaine lettuce with a sparkling mineral water for Nadine.

Nadine asked, "How is Carson doing these days? How's his mind?"

That had Vy frowning. "Some days are great, but today isn't one of them. I talked to Sam just before the lunch rush and Carson is tired and confused."

Someone called for coffee farther down the counter. Vy snagged a fresh pot and supplied refills along the counter. Soon, she was lost in a bustle of activity serving tables.

"How's the revival going?" Zach asked. "The rides look great."

"Rachel did an amazing job. Honey has the food ordered and the booths organized."

"I heard she hired a lot of local teenagers."

"Yes, and a bunch of the older women to make sure everything runs smoothly." She barely tasted the food. She wanted to have this business done, not sit here pretending everything was normal while Zach shot her puzzled looks. Why wouldn't he when she was acting like last night had never happened?

"Samantha's taking care of finances," she said. "She lets me know how much I can spend on advertising and promotion."

"And Max has the rodeo in hand?"

Nadine frowned. "Things aren't running as smoothly there as I'd like. I don't know…"

"It will work out, Nadine. Max is good people. She's responsible. She'll pull it together."

"I hope so."

He touched her hand, gently unfolding the two fingers she hadn't realized she'd crossed for luck.

"Things will work out." His confidence boosted her even as the touch of his hand unsettled her. He let go and she could breath again.

"This event *has* to be successful," she said, admitting the fears she didn't spread around town. The committee needed everyone to believe it would work. "The life of the town depends on it. We need the jobs and the income. Too many of our young people are leaving."

"Like you did."

Was there a hint of criticism in his tone, or was she imagining it? "Like I did," she admitted.

"Are you okay?" he murmured low. "I thought things would be good between us after last night, but you seem tense."

She tried to sound normal. "I'm just tired, I guess."

He smiled and ate. She liked his smile. It was natural and warm and, above all, honest. Oh, how Nadine's flimsy house of cards was about to crumble.

Fifteen minutes later, Nadine left the diner with Zach.

"Let's take my truck instead of two vehicles."

They drove out of town toward Norma's nursing home, a good twenty minutes on the other side of town. The interior of Zach's truck, messy with old coffee cups and chocolate bar wrappers, wrapped Nadine in a snug embrace.

As hard as Nadine struggled, she couldn't come up with a topic of conversation that would take them all the way to the seniors' home in the neighboring county.

She mentioned the weather, asked after the twins and his father.

Through it all, Zach answered in monosyllables. The guy could at least do his share of the work. After her next vapid comment, he slid an amused smile her way and said, "We don't *have* to talk, you know. We can just enjoy the ride."

That left Nadine uncomfortable. Last night had been amazing. This afternoon would be awful. Nadine didn't know how to lie, how to pretend to be normal when she thought she could predict what was about to happen when Norma saw Zach.

Or maybe—she crossed her fingers again—she was wrong. *Please, please, please be wrong, Nadine.* Maybe Norma would greet Zach vaguely and not give away what Nadine thought she knew.

They reached the nursing home, thank goodness, and Nadine scooted out of the truck the second it came to a stop.

She sensed more than heard Zach following her into the building. At the reception desk, she asked whether they could visit Norma Beeton and got the okay.

Nadine led Zach to her room, where Norma sat in a wheelchair beside a window.

She turned as they walked in. When she saw Zach she stared at him for a very long time. Then a broad smile lit her face. "Hello, Harvey."

Beside Nadine, Zach startled. Nadine held still.

The worst had happened. Zach's appearance had jogged Norma's memory, exactly as Nadine had suspected. *This* was the secret. Harvey had died so young that only people as old as Norma remembered what he'd looked like.

And Zach had inherited his features.

Rick didn't look like his father. He looked like his mother. The likeness had skipped a generation to manifest in Zach. By the time Zach had become an adult and the resemblance was obvious, most anyone who would have known would be Norma's age.

Zach hadn't been clued in to what was going on. He didn't know. He hadn't known.

"Haven't seen you around town lately, Harvey," Norma said, voice frail. "How's Judith?" At the mention of Zach's grandmother's name, an edge crept into Norma's tone.

Judith, the grandmother Zach had never met, and a huge part of a scandal?

Zach frowned, no doubt wondering why Norma would mention Harvey and Judith in the same sentence.

"It's Zach, Norma," he said. "Zach Brandt."

"No. No. Harvey, you're a Broome. Why would you say you're a Brandt? Who's Zach?"

Zach whipped around to stare at Nadine. Only slowly did she return his gaze.

Yes, she told him with her eyes, *I guessed. Oh, Zach, I'm so sorry.*

Norma started to talk without the least bit of a prompt from Nadine. "It's awful what Judith did to you, Harvey. But you do understand, don't you? You can't force love where it doesn't exist."

The lost look on Zach's face made him younger, like a little boy afraid of the dark. "I don't—" He foundered. "What are you talking about?"

He was the most straightforward, honest man Nadine had ever known. The task of understanding an old deception must be overwhelming him.

"Judith loves Richard," Norma said. "It's that simple.

I know when you came back from the war you tried to persuade her that she still loved you."

Norma shook her finger at Zach. "You shouldn't have pressured her into your bed, but she was trying hard to be right for you. To honor the commitment she had made to you before the war. You had the previous claim."

She stared at her hands. "The war changed all of you men, yes, but you've got to understand, Harvey, what it did to us women at home all alone and scared every single day that we would get bad news. We worked. We became independent. We became strong."

The sudden look she shot at Zach blazed with anger. "You wanted her to be exactly the same young, impressionable girl you'd left behind. *You* weren't the same. Why should she have been? That war killed pieces of every one of us. You couldn't accept change in Judith."

Her gaze became cagey again. "But Richard could. He loved Judith, every aspect of her. How could she not fall for all of that love and support and understanding?"

She watched Zach, waiting for him to answer. The longer he stood watching her mutely, the less sure she seemed of herself.

"Harvey?" She peered at Zach through narrowed eyes. "You're not Harvey, are you?"

"No, ma'am," Zach said stiffly. "I'm not a Broome. I'm a Brandt."

"You have the look of a Broome." Slowly, she blinked, as if coming out of a dream. "Oh, dear."

When Nadine used to see Norma at the paper ten years ago, the older woman's mind had been sharp. She'd been a smart woman. That woman peeked through.

Norma turned to Nadine. "What's going on?"

"This is Zach Brandt, Norma, but you just mistook him for Harvey Broome. Do you know why?"

"Of course I do. He's Harvey Broome's grandson."

"No!" The force of that one word from Zach seemed to shake the room.

Dismay flitted across Norma's features. "You didn't know? Does your father? Rick? Did his parents never tell him? I was the only one in town she told, but I'd thought they would have shared the truth with their son and grandson."

"Tell me everything," Zach said, expression unyielding. "Don't leave out anything."

The story poured from the old woman.

Harvey's first wife had given birth to a boy in the midthirties, during the depression, but she died shortly thereafter. He turned his attentions to Judith, but waited until after her sixteenth birthday to propose. He was a handsome and persuasive young man and she said yes.

"She was so young when she agreed to marry him," Norma continued. "Too young. When the men returned, Judith was twenty, more mature and changed. Harvey came home bitter, wanting things to be the way they used to be, but that was never going to happen. Judith saw how unhappy their marriage would be, even after one night—*especially* after one night—with Harvey."

Norma studied her hands. "You know, Judith really didn't want to sleep with Harvey, but as I said, he could be persuasive. Judith was trying to honor the promise she had made to him before the war. In the end, she couldn't. It took a lot of courage to walk away from Harvey. He was furious."

Apparently, when Judith turned to Richard, he'd married her immediately. Only afterward did they realize she'd already been pregnant with Harvey's baby. They raised Rick as their own.

"Then Harvey and Richard had that dreadful fight

after they married and Judith started to show. Harvey kept asking, is the baby mine? Is the baby mine?" She described that terrible night by the quarry.

"After that," Norma continued, "it seemed even more important to keep the secret about Rick's paternity or the town might think Richard had killed Harvey deliberately. Thank goodness I was there.

"I never told anyone. Not a soul. Not until now..." Her voice trailed off and she looked uncertain for a moment. Her expression clouded, the acuity they'd seen a second ago gone now. Her mind was no longer in the past, yet not quite here, and it all showed on her face.

Zach hung his head and swore softly.

"We should leave," Nadine whispered.

"Norma," she said. "Thank you for talking to us."

The older woman seemed worn out. But when she glanced at Zach, she brightened. "Harvey! It's good to see you."

Poor Norma. How confusing to have a mind that wouldn't stand still and that played tricks on her.

Zach said, "I have to go," and hurried from the room.

"Come visit again." Norma had lost her veneer of lucidity. She studied her room uncertainly. She swung her watery gaze to Nadine. "Come back. Okay?"

"Yes, of course, Norma." She meant it. Nadine promised she would get a nurse to help her into bed then headed outside. She found Zach leaning against the hood of his truck and breathing heavily.

"My entire life has been a lie. My identity has been a lie. I'm not a Brandt. I'm a Broome. I live, work and breathe on the Brandt ranch, but I'm not a Brandt."

Nadine held herself still, afraid of what he'd say next.

"You knew?" he asked, voice harsh.

"I saw an old photo of Harvey Broome when I was researching his death. I suspected."

"You brought me here knowing what would happen."

Regret flared in Nadine's chest and she stared at the ground. "Yes."

Zach straightened and she saw the understanding hit. "This is part of your article, isn't it?"

"Yes," she whispered.

"What? I didn't hear you."

She cleared her throat and spoke more loudly. "I said yes."

"My God." He swore fluently. "I thought you were a better woman, a better person, than *this*. You've been digging up dirt on my family."

She nodded. That had been exactly what she had been doing.

"I opened my home to you, you liar."

Nadine flinched. Zach didn't swear. He didn't bully. She'd brought him so low.

"The boys! My boys love you. They would like nothing better than to have you in their lives all the time." Zach pounded his fist on the hood. "I exposed them to a lie. To a woman who was bound to break their hearts."

Nadine still hadn't looked at him.

He leaned close. "I will never forgive you for this."

Her vision clouded with unshed tears.

"Why? Is journalism more important to you than your integrity? Is it more important than *people*?"

She looked at him then, finally meeting his eyes so she could explain. "It wasn't me. It was Lee. I was honest when I contacted you to ask for an interview. It was truly all about your artwork, about giving the locals a glimpse of you, not inside the rancher, but the artist."

"So why this?" His arm swung wide to indicate the

building behind them, where Norma was probably sleeping the sleep of the blameless.

"Lee told me I had to find out a secret that his mother knew. She wouldn't share it with him. And until today, I couldn't get it out of her, either."

"And you were so hungry for…what? A scoop? Isn't that what it's called? So you ran with it?"

"No! I told Lee that I wanted no part of this, but he was adamant. He said he needed to sell more papers. He said if I didn't dig up dirt and find out whatever this secret was that he would fire me." She clenched her fists. "I have nowhere else to go. If I don't have this job, I have nothing."

"You want to know something, Nadine?" He stepped close and loomed over her. His scent was familiar and precious to her, but anger rolled from him like smoke and fire. "I would have let Lee fire me and would live homeless before I would betray someone like you're betraying me. I would have told you in private and left it at that. I would live with nothing before hurting or exposing you. I would hit rock bottom before I would have betrayed you or any other person I love."

He loved her? He *loved* her?

Oh, dear God, what had she done? What *had* she done?

"There is no job on earth that is worth this betrayal." He pounded his chest with his fist. "There is no number of papers sold that makes up for the pain in here." Zach leaned over the engine and hung his head. "My grandmother made one mistake and now I no longer know my heritage. The core of who I am has always been my family and that ranch. My home."

"You *are* a Brandt, Zach."

He turned on her and hissed, "But I'm not, am I?"

"You are a Brandt in every way that matters." She argued as though her life depended on making everything better for him. "Your mother didn't make a mistake. She tried to honor an agreement. Afterward she realized it would never work. She married your grandfather before she knew she was pregnant. Her only mistake was in withholding that truth from Rick."

She touched his arm, but he pulled away. She *had* to convince him, to repair some of the damage done. "Richard raised Rick as his own son. He was truly his son in every way that mattered, as you are his grandson in every way that matters. The core of who you are is the good, good man you have always been, no matter the genes that created you. Brandts raised you to be the solid, wonderful man you are."

"I don't know who the hell I am." He strode to the driver's door of his truck. "I don't know who the hell *you* are. I thought I did. I thought I wanted you in my life, but you aren't the woman I admired. That woman was a figment of my lousy, overactive imagination."

He opened the door, but halted, struck by a thought. He asked despairingly, "Who are my sons?"

The truck moved violently when he got in and slammed the door. He backed out of the parking spot and drove away with a squealing of brakes.

Nadine had screwed up as badly as she had in New York City. She had put her wants and needs before someone else's and had ruined him.

Aunt Denise had been right along. Nadine was not and never would be a good person. She had just laid low a good man who was worth twenty of her.

I would have let Lee fire me and would live homeless before I would betray someone like you're betraying me.

That was Zach in a nutshell, a decent man with a

backbone of steel, and only now in this moment and much too late did Nadine realize how much she loved him.

She had just lost everything.

She stood on the pavement for a long time before realizing she would have to find her own way back to town.

Vy would be busy at the diner.

Honey would be busy with her new family.

Rachel had her hands full with her two girls.

So Nadine called Max.

Twenty minutes later, Max drove up in her old, filthy pickup truck and jumped out, her cowboy boots dusty and a plaid shirt coming untucked from her jeans.

"What's going on, Nadine? Car trouble?" With one look at Nadine's face, the smile slipped from Max's lips. "Get in," she ordered.

For the length of the drive, Nadine didn't say a word. Back in Rodeo, she got out of the truck and headed for her front door, but Max followed and blocked her path.

Without speaking, standoffish Max took Nadine into her arms and held on fiercely.

"When you're ready to talk," she whispered into Nadine's ear, "you call. Y'hear?"

Nadine nodded. Max let her go and drove off. Nadine climbed up her stairs, threw herself onto her bed and wept.

And wept.

She didn't stop for twelve hours.

ZACH SAT IN his truck in the yard staring at the house, the outbuildings, the fields—the home he'd thought was his, as a Brandt. As one in a long line of Brandts.

This was *his* land. *His* place on this earth. The one and only place he truly belonged.

In time, Pop came out of the house with the boys, who ran circles around the truck. "You going to get out anytime soon?" Rick asked. "The twins were asking what you're doing."

Zach turned in slow, miniscule increments to look at his father. He didn't know how to hide his devastation.

Rick's mouth dropped open. "What—?" To the boys, he said, "Aiden and Ryan, go to the stable and saddle up your ponies. You can ride the field but stay within sight of us, y'hear?"

They ran off, hooting.

Rick set his crooked hands on the window frame. "What's happened?"

"Did you know?"

"Know what?"

"About Harvey Broome?"

He frowned. "Tommy's grandfather? What about him? You're scaring me, boy. You look like hell. What's going on?"

Oh, God. His dad didn't know. How was Zach supposed to tell his father that his life had been a lie?

"We'd better… I need to… Aw, hell," Zach said. He nudged the door open and Rick stepped back. Zach got out and walked to the house.

They sat on the veranda. The boys rode out of the stable on their ponies and trotted into the field. Both father and grandfather would be able to keep an eye on them for a fair distance. For this treat of riding on their own, the boys would be good and not go too far.

"Did someone die?" Pop asked.

"No."

"Then what?"

Not knowing how to go on, Zach blurted what he had learned from Norma.

Rick didn't move for a very long time before saying, "I never knew."

"I'm sorry."

"So am I. Though I always thought there was something going on."

"Why would you think that?"

Rick stood and went into the house. He returned with a couple of cans of beer.

"Sometimes late at night, I'd hear my parents talk. Mom would be upset while Dad soothed her. More than once, I heard her ask him if they should tell me. I never knew what she meant. Dad carried on with life as if everything was fine."

He took a long pull on the can.

"I'll tell you one thing. I never felt unloved. With his dying breath, your grandfather told me how much he loved me and that I was the best thing that ever happened to him."

"Then you were."

Rick sniffed and Zach wondered if his dad was crying. He stared out at the yard. He wouldn't embarrass his dad by remarking on it.

After a while, Rick said, "Then I was. He was a man who told the truth. He taught me to do the same and I passed those lessons on to you. If my dad said he loved me, then he did."

For the next hour, they watched the twins ride the land with gleeful abandon, blissfully ignorant of the crisis happening in their home.

Chapter Ten

Through the following week, Nadine stayed in her apartment. She missed the twins, and Zach, with an ache that had her doubling over and clutching her knees.

When she'd left New York, she'd thought it was the worst she could feel in her life. She hadn't known she could fall lower still. But she had.

And she couldn't stop, tumbling head over heels into despair.

She refused to answer email, texts, her phone, the doorbell.

She knew Lee expected an article, but she ignored him, too. Let him rant and rave. She didn't care.

On the fifth day, she heard a key in her lock downstairs and several pairs of feet climbing to her apartment.

Vy entered first, followed by the rest of the revival committee. They stopped and stared.

"Dear God," Vy whispered. "What have you done to yourself?"

"Told you she was bad," Max said. With a hard glare, she continued, "But I didn't think she was this bad."

Honey squatted in front of Nadine where she lay curled in a fetal position on the sofa. "Nadine, sweetie, what's happened to you? I've never seen you less than perfect. Same goes for this apartment. It's a pigsty."

Nadine shrugged.

"You need a shower," Max accused.

Nadine heard Vy on the phone. "Will, I need soup. Lots of it. Bring whatever comfort food you have ready. I'm at Nadine's. Call when you leave. I'll meet you at the door." She ended the call, then ordered, "Into the shower."

"No," Nadine whispered.

"You stink, dear," Rachel said.

"I don't care."

"I do," Vy said and she and Honey, strong from the work they did in the diner and the bar, took her by both arms and all but dragged her to the bathroom.

"You can do this alone," Vy said, "or we can strip you and bathe you ourselves."

Nadine stared at her friends. It was no idle threat. They would do it. "Go," she whispered. "Get out. I'll wash myself."

"Your hair, too?" Honey stared. "God, I've never seen you with dirty hair before."

"I'll clean it."

Vy pointed a finger at her. "We're trusting you. If you don't come out clean in twenty minutes, we're coming in."

Nadine nodded and they left her sitting on the side of the tub. Honey returned with a clean outfit, dropped it onto Nadine's lap and closed the door behind her.

Nadine sat in the ensuing silence, overwhelmed by the supportive whirlwind that was her friends.

She stared in the mirror at the woman she barely recognized.

You are perfectly, sublimely you.

Not so sublime at the moment, was she?

When she emerged twenty minutes later washed,

flossed, brushed and clean, her apartment had been tidied as well. All traces of the boxes of tissues she'd used had been thrown out. The old food she'd left in pots had been tossed. Her kitchen was spick and span. She heard the laundry machine turn on.

Honey walked down the hallway. "I just put your bed sheets in. We'll have a clean bed for you in no time."

All of the windows were open and a fresh breeze rushed down the length of the hallway.

Vy handed her a cup of coffee. "Sit. Talk."

Nadine sipped it and sank heavily onto the sofa. She set the mug on the coffee table, noticed her missing treasures and wailed, "Where are they?"

No!

She jumped up from the sofa, scrabbling through the tidy pile of magazines in front of her. "Where are they? What have you done? Oh, please tell me you didn't throw them out!"

Rachel took her arm and asked, voice as gentle as her touch, "What are you looking for?"

The no-nonsense, loving concern in her voice calmed Nadine somewhat, but fear leaked through in her voice. "The boys gave me such sweet little things. They're all I have left of their love."

Honey approached with her hands cupped in front of her. There on her palms sat a small yellow Monopoly house, a tiny china teacup and a little sleeping cat figurine.

Max handed her the small pile of notes they'd given her, clues to a mystery that had probably never existed. All they'd wanted was for her to visit again.

Nadine took them from Honey, held them against her chest and started to cry.

Honey urged her back to the sofa. "Oh, sweetie, you need to talk to us."

"What boys gave you those?" Vy asked.

"Must've been Zach's twins. Boys are more affectionate than you think." Max had a small son so she understood.

"Yes," Nadine whispered. "They are so sweet." Her breathing hitched and she stood. "I'll never see them again." She started to cry in earnest.

"Sit," Vy ordered, and Nadine did.

"You need to eat," Honey said.

"In a minute." Nadine's voice came out as a dry old croak. She sipped her hot coffee and started again. "I have so much to tell you." And she did while she clutched her small treasures in one fist and their clues in the other fist against her chest, near her heart.

She started with her intention to do a straight story about Zach, the painter. She explained what Lee had pressured her into digging up. She did not share the details of what she'd discovered. She owed Zach that much.

He had been right. He would never have compromised anyone around him for personal gain, no matter the threat to his livelihood.

Amid all of the ensuing sympathy, one person's voice rang louder than the others. Max.

"How are you going to fix this?"

"I don't know if I can, Max. Zach must hate me."

"Probably. I would."

"Max!" Honey said.

"Be quiet! Hush!" Vy and Rachel chimed in.

"No, Nadine already knows the truth in her heart," Max insisted. "She can't move forward in her life without fixing this, one way or another." She stood in front of Nadine. "You have to either write the article and have

Zach hate you forever, or refuse to write it and lose your job and the newspaper."

"*That's* going to make her feel a lot better," Samantha said.

Honey shook her head. "Max, how could you—?"

"She's right." Nadine interrupted everyone's protests. "Max is absolutely right. I can't hide here any longer. I need to make a decision and follow through on it."

There was a surprised silence until Vy asked, "So what's your decision?"

Tears flooded Nadine's eyes, but she forced them back. She'd cried enough. It was time for action. She just wished she knew what that action might be.

"You should—" Rachel started, but Max shushed her.

"Nadine already knows what she should do." She leaned forward, hands on her knees, and got into Nadine's face. Her thick, dark braid swung forward over her shoulder. "You know what you have to do, don't you?" Hard-edged, rough-and-tumble Max spoke with such a sweet tenderness that Nadine was speechless for a moment. It was the voice Max normally reserved for her son.

Oh. *Oh*. Despite everything, Max still loved her.

"Yes, Max, I do know what I have to do." Nadine turned to Violet. "Vy?"

"Yes, sweetie?"

"Do you need a waitress or a dishwasher?"

"Not at the moment, but we can find something for you. You won't starve."

"Not physically, no." But her psyche would wither without journalism.

"It'll be a sacrifice, Nadine," Max said. "But sometimes sacrifice is the only right way to go."

Nadine smiled grimly. "I know, Max." She straightened her spine. "I'm hungry."

Five women jumped to prepare food for her. They also shared in all of the excess that Will had brought over from the diner.

How on earth had Nadine left these beautiful people to live in New York? How had she managed to survive those years without them?

With loneliness.

Only now could she admit that while she'd been fired up for her career she had also been as lonely as hell. She'd done nothing but work.

She might not have a job in her beloved journalism come tomorrow, but she had a home here in Rodeo, in the collective bosom of the best friends a woman could have.

After the women left, Nadine took a long hard look at her life and her choices. She didn't deserve a relationship with any man, let alone with one as full of integrity as Zach. Zach would have never destroyed another person for any reason, not even if he feared losing his job.

Nadine had felt unworthy for two decades ever since moving in with her aunt and living with her constantly putting Nadine down.

She had always blamed her aunt and rightly so.

But not this time. This time Nadine had screwed up royally. It was all her fault. She couldn't blame Denise. She couldn't blame the early loss of her mother's love. She was old enough to make herself into a healthier person.

She had let herself be ruled by fear.

Once before she had made a mistake where another person's well-being was concerned and he had died. Zach had been right in that young James had made his own decision to take his life, but Nadine had not taken care to help him more.

She had been careless again and someone else would suffer. Zach would suffer. So would Rick. So would those sweet little boys.

The moment Lee had threatened her with being fired, she should have told him she wouldn't destroy a good man and his worthy family.

She should have quit and walked out with her dignity intact. Instead she had compromised herself and her core values. It was time to pull herself up by her bootstraps, take full responsibility and make amends.

She had only the most vague clue of how to do that, but an idea was forming.

For the next couple of days she wrote her article, promising Lee she would submit it to part-timer David, who would format and send off to the printers in time for publication and that Lee would be delighted with the secret about Zach's family.

"You aren't kidding?" Lee rubbed his hands.

"I'm not kidding, Lee. I will disclose the secret."

"Tell me."

Nadine smiled as though they already shared that secret. "Trust me, Lee. It will be worth the wait."

She wrote an article about Zach the artist and handed it in to David, who had no idea there was supposed to be more. Back up in her apartment, she waited until almost the last minute and emailed David to tell him she'd given him the wrong version of the article.

She emailed the correct version.

After printing up a copy, she laid it neatly into a folder and drove out to Zach's ranch, the most difficult thing she'd ever done in her life.

ZACH SAT ON the side of his mountain—no, *not* his mountain—and stared out across *not* his land. A week later, he still hadn't come to terms with who or what he was.

The boys had picked up on his unhappiness. They were reckless and moody.

Why had Tommy Broome never said, "You look like my grandfather?" Didn't that family keep photo albums like Zach's did? Didn't the guy ever look at them?

Apparently not.

He saw Nadine when she was still a long distance off. Every particle, every cell and sinew of his body froze. She rode closer and closer, taking her time on sweet little Butter. Pop must have told her where he was.

What had she said to Rick to convince him to do so? To let her saddle up one of *his* horses? She had a lot of nerve showing her face here.

That night in the cabin when she'd confessed her story about James, she had said she didn't deserve forgiveness and benediction and grace.

He had believed in her better nature. He'd convinced her that she did deserve it all.

He'd been wrong and she had been right. She didn't deserve forgiveness. She was not the woman he'd thought she was.

He couldn't believe he'd had a crush on her in high school. Had she been different then, or had she always had this capacity for betrayal inside her? How could he have thought an unethical woman like her could be his second chance at love?

What a fool he'd been.

The fury flushing his body would be violent if it weren't tamped by the depression that had hit from the moment Norma Beeton had said, "Hello, Harvey."

It brought back all of Zach's feelings of betrayal after he'd married Maria only to find out she hadn't been honest with him. She'd wanted to change him.

She hadn't succeeded.

But Nadine had. She had changed Zach fundamentally. She had shown him that he belonged nowhere, that all of this beautiful land around him shouldn't be his.

He was not a Brandt. He was a Broome. Which meant he would have to talk to Tommy at some point about all of this, especially once the article came out. And why hadn't it been published already?

Nadine headed for the cabin until she saw him sitting on the promontory he called his "armchair."

Don't, he wanted to shout. *Don't come near me*. He didn't want her close enough to touch.

Changing direction, she approached, her face shadowed by a broad-brimmed straw hat. When she dismounted, her hair swung in a long, straight braid over her shoulder. She took off her hat and held it in one hand while she held Butter's reins in the other.

Her eyes, he noted, were sunken. She looked tired. Exhausted. So. She hadn't slept this past week, either. Guilt? Certainly not remorse. She'd gotten what she'd first come here for. Dirt. Scandal.

"Did you really hate me so much?" He hadn't meant to speak.

She winced as though he'd slapped her, but she didn't leave or step back. She should. There was no telling what he might say in his current mood.

"I don't hate you, Zach," she said, her voice rough. "Never. I admire you."

"You have a strange way of showing it." His jaw hurt. He'd been clenching his teeth for a week.

"May I sit?"

A hard shake of his head was the full sum of his response.

"If I drop the reins, will Butter run away?"

"No." He wished Butter *would* run, though, so Nadine would have to walk all the way back to her car.

She dropped the reins and her hat to the ground. With a start he realized she wasn't wearing makeup. Not a speck. Freckles, dark circles under her eyes, every faint flaw on nearly perfect skin laid bare for all to witness.

Shrugging out of a backpack, she unzipped it and took out a manila envelope.

She handed it to him, but he refused to take it. Why would he? He didn't want to touch anything she'd laid a hand to. He didn't even like her using his horse.

Her hands shook. In fact, a fine tremor ran through her body. It must have taken courage to come here.

He didn't want to think of her in positive terms. He didn't want to acknowledge she could possibly be good in any way.

What the heck *had* she said to Rick for him to send her out here on Butter?

Zach's father's world had been blown apart, too. He'd been in a daze. He'd been shaken. They had gone through every paper in their small ranch office. They'd scoured the attic for anything that might pertain to the Broomes. Nothing. Rick's father truly had accepted him as his own, as a Brandt, and that was that.

But both Rick and Zach knew the truth now. What was it worth? Zach didn't know.

Nadine placed the envelope on the rock beside him, leaning close enough for her scent to whisper around him. It wasn't the light floral scent she usually wore. She smelled like fabric softener.

Had she thought that by dressing down he might take her more seriously?

"Well," she said and watched him for any sign of reaction.

There was none. His face felt frozen. *He* was frozen.

She mounted and rode away. He watched her straight back and long red braid until she was a tiny speck.

He glanced down at the envelope.

Nope. He wouldn't touch it. It could sit here in the elements and rot for all he cared. For another hour, he ignored it until the thing seemed to grow and glow in his peripheral vision.

With a pungent oath, he picked it up and opened it. He drew out a sheaf of papers.

On top was a letter of resignation addressed to Lee Beeton and signed by Nadine Campbell.

What the hell?

He read through the single paragraph telling the man that she could no longer work for him because the journalism he demanded of her was not the journalism with which she wanted to be associated.

She finished with one line.

I would rather be a dishwasher and take out the garbage.

But? He flipped through the papers. The letter was accompanied by an article.

There was something here that Zach wasn't getting. She had tendered her resignation, but had written the article anyway? What ridiculous point was the woman trying to make?

I'll become a better person, I will develop backbone and integrity, after *I publish the article?*

His fingers burned where they touched the bundle. The first line caught his eye.

What did it mean?
He read further:

Let me tell you a love story.

It involves war and separation and growth…and the realization of truth.

Once truth and love have been acknowledged, they can't be denied, not even in a small town in a time of strict morals and narrow life choices.

Love transcends promises made by adolescents who are merely children at heart, children who are forced to go off to war and who are forged into adulthood in the hottest crucible of hell.

Some came home whole and some came home broken. Waiting at home was insecurity, not-quite betrayal and blossoming love.

Let me tell you a story about courage, and what it took for a young woman to make the right choice no matter the cost.

BY THE TIME Zach finished reading, his vision had blurred a number of times. He swiped his thumbs beneath his eyes.

Four pages about love and courage. Nadine had written one hell of a story.

She hadn't named names, but the townspeople and everyone in the surrounding county would know who she was talking about. With such a…*tender* treatment of the subject, not a single person would think it was a juicy scandal.

Beyond a shadow of a doubt, Nadine had redeemed herself. Was it enough for him?

Rick had to see this.

Zach took Paintbrush out of the shed and rode back to the ranch house.

As they'd done a long, long week ago, the boys rode their ponies out into the field while Zach and Rick sat on the veranda.

"Read this," Zach said.

Rick pulled a pair of reading glasses out of his shirt pocket and put them on, carefully, avoiding touching the papers for as long as possible.

When he could delay no longer, he took them and read.

It took him a while.

Zach sat and looked out over land that he was willing to admit again belonged to him and his father. In his will, Richard Brandt had left everything to his son. Rick would leave it all to Zach. Parents weren't solely a set of DNA and genes. They were the people who raised you and loved you and shaped you. Nadine's article had reminded him of that.

Richard and Judith had done a bang-up job with Rick, who had married a lovely woman named Lisa who, along with Rick, had loved Zach to distraction until her death fourteen years ago.

After Rick finished reading, he set the article down on the small wicker table in front of them and cleared his throat once. Twice. Three times.

"Well. That was…"

Zach waited him out.

"That was something else." Rick took a large white handkerchief from his pocket and blew his nose. "Hell. It was beautiful."

"Yeah."

"I've been angry with my mother. I've even, in my mind, cursed her for not telling me the truth. For sleeping with a man she wasn't married to. Was she a loose woman?"

"You know she wasn't," Zach asserted. "She was young and confused. She'd made a boy a promise when she was only a girl. He'd come home angry, devastated by war and expecting her to be someone she wasn't. Your *true* father, Richard, loved and respected her."

Zach picked up the article and held it in a squashing grip. "Nadine must have talked to Norma again. Norma must have remembered more. There's a lot of detail here I didn't hear last week."

"She must have. There's lots you didn't tell me."

"I wonder what kind of backlash there'll be."

"Against us?" Rick asked.

"Yeah." Zach stood. "There's only one way to find out."

"What do you mean?"

"That paper came out this morning. We need to enter the lion's den."

"How exactly do we do that?"

Zach grinned. "We go to Vy's for lunch. We sit in a window booth if we can get one and we show everyone in town that we are proud to be Brandts."

Rick smiled. "We can do that."

With a sharp whistle, Rick caught the attention of the twins and waved them home.

Home, Zach thought. That precious word and even more precious concept. Rick had had a wonderful home here. So had Zach. So did his boys.

They trotted their ponies into the yard and whooped when Rick told them they were going into town for lunch.

Arriving in the diner about fifteen minutes before the rush, the four Brandts climbed into a window booth.

Vy came over to serve them with a wide, red-lipped

smile. "Glad to see you here. Good for you. If I hear one single word of malicious judgment, I'll clock someone."

Before Zach could sit, she gave him a rib-crushing hug. *Goddamn.* With a friend like Vy standing beside him, he could withstand the malice of any number of busybodies.

The diner filled up. Zach felt the weight of too many eyes on them.

Slowly, as people finished their lunches, they wandered to the Brandt table, every one of them saying hello and shooting the breeze as though it were a normal day. With their deliberate nonchalance, they offered acceptance and respect.

Zach struggled.

He'd never thought of himself as an emotional man, but these people… The esteem shown by these amazing, solid citizens could make any man cry.

It looked like Rick felt the same way.

After lunch, Vy brought suckers for the boys and insisted on hugs and kisses before she would hand them over. They did so happily. What person in his right mind could resist Violet Summer and her generous affection?

Zach drove them all home and onto the ranch that somehow the people of Rodeo had helped him to reclaim as his own. His heritage.

He rode an ATV out onto the range to catch up on all the work he'd let slide in the past week.

It felt good and right to be back on his family's land.

NADINE STOOD IN the newspaper office and let Lee Beeton rant, this morning's copy of the paper crushed in his fist.

She didn't care. Nothing much mattered anymore.

Too late, only after she'd lost Zach's respect, did she realize how deeply she loved him. She'd fallen head over heels. If she searched the world over for the rest of her life, she would never find a man more worthy of love and esteem and the best a person had to give.

Her heart and soul ached. Physically burned.

When Lee yelled, "You're fired!" she countered with, "You can't fire me. I quit."

She pointed to the letter of resignation on his desk. "I resigned." Hand on the doorknob, she turned back to face him. "When I was a teenager, you gave me my first chance. I will always remember and appreciate that. But what you did now was wrong." She opened the door. "You should have never threatened me. I should have never given in. Goodbye, Lee."

She stood on Main Street, tired and uncertain, but also buoyed with the knowledge that she had done her best in the end.

She unlocked her front door. Someone had slipped an envelope through her letter slot. She nearly stepped on it. She picked it up and carried it upstairs to her living room.

There, standing in a beam of sunlight streaming through the window, she slid a card out of the envelope, all glittery and gaudy. She peeked inside. It was from the Brandt boys and men, requesting the pleasure of her presence for dinner at the ranch that evening.

It had to be for forgiveness, right? They wouldn't invite her out there for dinner just to give her hell. Would they?

She closed the card and held it to her lips. When she pulled it away, some of the glitter came off on her mouth and she laughed.

The boys must have chosen the card. She would cherish it forever.

She studied everything in her closet and decided on the pretty outfit she'd worn to the tea party. After showering, she left her hair to dry in curls. She applied mascara and eye shadow and a pretty pink lipstick that matched her top. She left her freckles exposed.

Out on Main Street, prepared to walk down to the diner to see if Vy had a pie she could buy, Nadine was stopped by Lee.

"I need you." He stood humbly, eyes on the ground, as though subservient.

What the heck?

He invited her into the office. Curious, she followed.

He apologized and offered her back her job.

His rueful glance slid away from her. "I needed to sell papers. I'm so close to losing everything I worked so hard for over the years. Financially, the business is in trouble." His voice broke. "A lot of trouble."

Agitated, he paced between the window and his desk. "I even mortgaged my house last year. That was my mother's house. There hasn't been a mortgage on it since 1956." Anger crept into his voice. "Can you imagine? After the risk my father took in starting this business on his own and building it into a success, and after a lifetime of work on my part, I might lose it."

Nadine took a deep breath. She felt for the man, but he needed to hear some hard truths. "The industry has been in steady decline for years, Lee. If I can be frank, you haven't kept up with the times. You're running the paper as though we still live in the sixties or seventies." She glanced around the office. "Sure, we have computers, but other than that, you'd never know anything's changed in at least thirty, forty years. You need to become digital. You need to embrace technology. You *can* save this paper, Lee."

She had tried to tell him all of this before.

"No, I can't." He sighed. "But *you* can. I'm tired. I

can't stand the stress anymore. I want you to take over the *Rodeo Wrangler*."

Take over. Exactly what she wanted. She could write those articles about the seniors in Sunrise Home. She could judge stories written by the children of town for the contest.

A dream come true.

Could it be coming true even though she'd screwed up so badly with Zach?

Thinking of Zach, she knew she didn't deserve this.

But he'd invited her for dinner.

She rubbed her aching temples.

The phone rang and Lee answered. "Yes. It was a great article, wasn't it? Yes, I'll get her to write more just like it."

He hung up. "The phone's been ringing off the hook. You're a good writer, Nadine. When you write from the heart, you're spectacular."

"Were you serious about me running the paper?"

"Yes. I want to retire and stop worrying. I want you to take over and bring it up to date. Make it current. I don't want to leave you with a big financial mess, but going digital should cut costs. The way you've raised funds and promoted for the revival committee, I don't have a doubt you'll be able to make this business profitable again."

Nadine studied him. "Do I have carte blanche?"

"Yeah. You sure do. It seems that you know this business better than I do."

Nadine held out her hand. "Let's shake on it."

They did and Nadine left the office happier than she'd been in the past year that she'd worked there.

At the diner, she bought a coconut cream pie, placed it

lovingly on the front passenger seat and drove out to the Brandt ranch with her pulse beating wildly in her throat.

She didn't have a clue what she was about to face.

Chapter Eleven

She pulled into the yard slowly in case the boys were about.

Zach stood on the veranda watching her with a serious intensity that echoed that first day she'd come here to interview him.

She approached him. He stepped down.

"Nadine."

"Zach."

In another eerie echo of that first meeting, he lunged for her, but this time it wasn't to put her into ill-fitting, mismatched boots, but to lift her into his arms and twirl her around.

What—? Was she *forgiven*?

She squealed. "Zach! Oh, Zach, I've missed you."

"Have you?" He gazed into her eyes. "I missed you, too, even when I was angry."

"I'm so sorry," she whispered.

"Don't be." He set her back down on her feet. "You redeemed yourself. That article was beautiful."

"It was the least I could do. I was so wrong before."

"Yes, you were, but you came around beautifully. Nadine, I—"

Whatever he'd been about to say was lost amid the

whoops of two small boys running out of the house. They threw themselves against Nadine.

"You came back!"

"You're here."

"Yes, Ryan and Aiden, I'm here." She met Zach's dark warm gaze. "And I would like to stay."

Hope arose in her, clogging her throat.

"Boys," Zach said. "Step away from Nadine for a minute. There's something I need to do."

They stepped back and watched their father curiously.

Zach went down on one knee in front of Nadine. She gasped. He pulled a small box out of his pocket. "Will you marry me?"

Nadine covered her mouth with both hands.

The boys whooped again and fell to their knees. "Marry us, too!"

"We love you, too."

"Oh, you wonderful boys." She met Zach's loving gaze. "You wonderful man. How can I possibly say no?"

"Really, Nadine?"

She nodded. "Yes, really. I love all of you."

Rick spoke up from his spot on the veranda. "I remember you coming for a visit with your class and not liking this ranch very much." A faint accusation rumbled through his voice.

Nadine spent a moment taking in the house, the barn, the acres of land. Zach's mountain. It was hard to meet Rick's glare, but she did, directly. "I do now, Rick. I love it. I love your son. I love your grandchildren. I can't think of anything on this earth I would rather do more than live here and love here."

Rick smiled and she knew he had forgiven her, too.

With a small boy on either side of her hampering her

movement, she stepped toward the house. "Boys, about that mystery?"

"Yeah?"

"I never really saw a mystery. I just saw notes and clues that kept me coming out to the ranch."

"It worked, didn't it?"

"Yes, Ryan, those clues sure worked."

"You're here forever."

"Yes, Aiden, I am." How could she not have been able to tell them apart when they were such unique little boys?

Zach squeezed his sons' shoulders and gently pried them off her. "My turn. I've waited long enough. Go help Pop with dinner. I need to welcome Nadine to our ranch."

"We can welcome her, too."

"Not the way I'm going to."

The boys giggled and ran away.

Zach took Nadine into his arms and kissed the daylights out of her, welcoming her home. She kissed him right back, welcoming him into the promise of a loving, lifelong embrace.

When he came up for air, Zach whispered, "I'm going to count them, you know. After the boys go to bed tonight."

"Count what?"

He touched one finger to her nose. "Your freckles."

"That might take all night."

"Good."

"They don't end, you know. They're all over my entire body."

Zach smiled. "I know. I noticed, but I didn't have time to count them before."

He kissed her ear. "I'm going to love every freckle."

His breath warmed her throat. "I'm going to love every inch of you."

Just before kissing her lips, he said, "I'm going to love every perfect, sublime particle that is you, Nadine Campbell."

She smiled and gave herself over to love.

* * * * *

Catch up on all the romance in
Rodeo, Montana, with Mary Sullivan's
RODEO SHERIFF, RODEO BABY and more!
Visit Harlequin.com for a full list of titles.

We hope you enjoyed this story from
Harlequin® Western Romance.

Harlequin® Western Romance is coming to an
end, but community, cowboys and true love are
here to stay. Starting July 2018, discover more
heartfelt tales of family and friendship from
Harlequin® Special Edition.

Romance is for life, and these stories show that
every chapter in a relationship has its challenges
and delights and that love can be
renewed with each turn of the page!

Look for six *new* romances every month
from **Harlequin® Special Edition!**
Available wherever books are sold.

Get 4 FREE REWARDS!

We'll send you 2 FREE Books plus 2 FREE Mystery Gifts.

Harlequin® Special Edition books feature heroines finding the balance between their work life and personal life on the way to finding true love.

FREE Value Over $20

YES! Please send me 2 FREE Harlequin® Special Edition novels and my 2 FREE gifts (gifts are worth about $10 retail). After receiving them, if I don't wish to receive any more books, I can return the shipping statement marked "cancel." If I don't cancel, I will receive 6 brand-new novels every month and be billed just $4.99 per book in the U.S. or $5.74 per book in Canada. That's a savings of at least 12% off the cover price! It's quite a bargain! Shipping and handling is just 50¢ per book in the U.S. and 75¢ per book in Canada*. I understand that accepting the 2 free books and gifts places me under no obligation to buy anything. I can always return a shipment and cancel at any time. The free books and gifts are mine to keep no matter what I decide.

235/335 HDN GMY2

Name (please print)

Address   Apt. #

City   State/Province   Zip/Postal Code

Mail to the **Reader Service:**
IN U.S.A.: P.O. Box 1341, Buffalo, NY 14240-8531
IN CANADA: P.O. Box 603, Fort Erie, Ontario L2A 5X3

Want to try two free books from another series! Call 1-800-873-8635 or visit www.ReaderService.com.

SPECIAL EXCERPT FROM

◆ HARLEQUIN®

Western Romance

She's from New York City. He's a Montana rancher.
But they've got something special between them...

Read on for a sneak preview of
FALLING FOR THE REBEL COWBOY,
*part of the **COWBOYS TO GROOMS** series*
by Allison B. Collins!

Wyatt Sullivan stared at the beauty on the grass, glistening in the Montana sun. He knew each part of her intimately—he'd had his hands on every inch of her more times than he could count. With some pampering and TLC, he would get her purring beneath him again. After all, they didn't make tractors like this nowadays.

Click, click, click echoed on the concrete path from the lodge. A woman crossed into his line of sight, wearing a pink jacket molded to her sleek body and a matching skirt ending midthigh. Then her sharp words became clear.

"I was a fool to have married you. I should have listened to my father from the beginning. But we're divorced, and I'm stronger and smarter now. I won't let you treat our son like he doesn't matter."

The path curved, but she must have been distracted with her phone call, because she stepped off the concrete, still giving her ex a tongue-lashing. She was heading for the dirt of the soon-to-be vegetable garden. The one currently filled with mud from the heavy rain last night.

He had to grin as she tried to walk across the grass, her fancy pink heels sinking down with every step. She stumbled and lurched like a newborn foal trying to gain its legs.

"Ma'am, you might want—"

She flung a hand up at him and continued berating her ex on the phone.

"Watch out!" he called.

She turned around, glanced up at him and stepped back, midtirade. The ice pick heel on her fancy pink shoe snapped. She teetered back, her arms windmilling faster and faster and faster.

He sprinted toward her and grabbed for her hand but missed, snatching nothing more than air.

She landed on her back, spread-eagled, in the mud.

Her cell phone plopped in front of him. He picked it up and heard a man's voice still yelling. "She'll get back to you later," he said, then ended the call.

She glared, her pretty blue eyes narrowed at him. It wouldn't have surprised him if the ground beneath her started bubbling and boiling like a big pot of stew.

He smothered a laugh. "Hope you enjoy your mud bath, compliments of Sullivan Guest Ranch. Ma'am."

Don't miss FALLING FOR THE REBEL COWBOY
by Allison B. Collins,
available June 2018 wherever
Harlequin® books and ebooks are sold.

www.Harlequin.com

Looking for more satisfying love stories
with community and family at their core?

Check out **Harlequin® Special Edition**
and **Harlequin® Western Romance** books!

New books available every month!

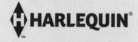